Yellow Lines

Jon Wesick

WESICK,
J.

This is a work of fiction. Names, characters, places, and incidents either are the product of the author's imagination or are used fictitiously. Any resemblance to actual persons, living or dead, events, or locales is entirely coincidental.

ACKNOWLEDGMENTS

I wish to thank my writing teachers Sam Hamod and Glory Foster, all those who commented on my work through many years of read and critique sessions, as well as Jim Babwe for his editing.

CHAPTER 1

The day his father sabotaged Grady Evans's future started out well. Because Grady had aced the last test, he got to spend a period in the library instead of enduring the review in American Government. Mr. Anderson let the trig class out at 2:00 after assigning only a half-dozen problems. Since Grady was a senior, he qualified for early release from high school and could spend a few hours studying at Marisol's house before he had to be at aikido.

He put the beige, trig textbook in his backpack and slammed his locker. As Grady walked down the hall toward the parking lot, a football player, 280 pounds of beef in a letter jacket, clapped him on the shoulder.

"Tell your mom to keep fighting, Grady."

"Will do."

It was a sunny day in May 2002 with temperatures in the low seventies. The winter rains had ended in April and the gloom that blankets Encinitas, California in late spring had not yet arrived. With its peeling paint and rust spots filled with flat red Bond-O, Grady's boxy Volvo 740 looked as out of place as a plate of macaroni and cheese at a five-star restaurant when compared with the other students' SUVs and racing Honda's. The aging clutch slipped, causing the car to jerk as Grady inched out of the parking lot.

After a ten-minute drive, he parked on the street in front of Marisol's house. Her brown Saturn was in the driveway with its hood open. As he approached, Grady spotted a pair of legs in blue, polyester pants protruding from under the Saturn's front end. He tiptoed closer for a better view. The baggy, grease-stained slacks hung low on Marisol's narrow frame, exposing her flat belly and the graceful curve of her hips. A grunt and a bang came from under the car.

"Shit!" Marisol crawled out from underneath with a grimy oil filter in her hands. She set it down, brushed away a lock of licorice-colored hair that had come loose from under her bandanna, and left a smudge on her forehead. "This will just take a minute." She pecked Grady on the lips and wiggled under the car with a new filter.

After adding several quarts of oil to the crankcase, Marisol led

Grady inside and past a picture of the Virgin of Guadalupe. The olive-skinned virgin wore a star-studded blue cloak and with head bowed and hands in prayer stood in her picture frame on the wooden ledge next to a pair of votive candles.

"Marisol, don't forget to clean up. We have dinner at your sister's, tonight." Marisol's mother came out of the kitchen. "Oh hi, Grady. How's your mom?"

"Not so good, Mrs. Ortiz. The doctors put her on a new course of chemo and she's not taking it well."

"Why don't you have her see my acupuncturist? When I was having trouble with my sciatica he gave me these magnets to use…" Mrs. Ortiz put her hand over her mouth. "Oh, listen to me ramble. Why don't you two go study? I'll find Dr. Chang's card for you."

Grady bounded up the carpeted stairs after Marisol but stepped aside to make way for the dark-haired boy rushing the other direction.

"How you doing, Eduardo?"

The child nodded at Grady and kept going. Grady and Marisol entered her bedroom. At first, this had seemed odd to him but Mrs. Ortiz didn't appear to mind as long as the door stayed open.

"I've got some good news." Marisol wrapped her arms around Grady and kissed him.

The backpack slid from his shoulder. Grady reached under her baggy denim shirt, ran his hands over the smooth skin of her back, and fumbled with the hook on her bra.

"Grady!" Marisol wiggled out of his grasp as if she were a diver escaping a giant squid's tentacles. "Don't you want to hear my news?"

"All right."

"Mom says I can get a single room at the dorm next fall. Do you know what that means?" She tugged his hands and studied his face. "We can spend the night together without having to deal with my roommate."

He kissed her.

"Grady, I have to study." Marisol sat cross-legged on the chair at her desk and opened a new copy of *Gray's Anatomy*.

"What are you looking at?" He came up behind her and rested a hand on her shoulder.

"The stages of an embryo." Marisol pointed to a drawing that looked like a seahorse. "This one's three weeks old."

"Why don't you relax a bit?" Grady bent forward and touched his lips to the caramel skin on the back of her neck. "Your classes don't start until fall."

Marisol's eyelids fluttered for a moment before she recovered. "Anatomy's going to be my hardest course. I don't want to get stuck spending an extra year doing prerequisites before transferring to the Midwifery Institute. Did you get your acceptance letter from the University of Washington?"

"Still no word."

"It's early. With your SAT scores, they'll have to let you in. Now, don't you have some homework?"

Grady did a few problems with tangents and sines but lost interest in the word problem about a boat steering across a current. The black-and-white drawings of triangles in his textbook were no competition for the warm flesh of the woman nearby. Absorbed in the urgency of their bodies, they lost track of time until Mrs. Ortiz's footsteps sounded on the stairs. Grady and Marisol straightened their clothes and rushed back to their books.

"We have to get ready for dinner at your sister's." Mrs. Ortiz turned to Grady and handed him a card. "Here's Dr. Chang's number. I hope it helps."

In spite of her husband's entreaties, Grady's mother, Rowan Walker-Evans, continued smoking the cigarettes that had made her ill. "What are they going to do, give me lung cancer?" she always said. She was polite about it and always went out on the patio before lighting up. That's where Grady found her. He'd opened the refrigerator and was about to reach for the mozzarella when a whiff of demon tobacco dug its noxious claws into his nostrils. He entered the family room and looked out the sliding-glass door.

Eyes closed, his mother was nodding her head to the sounds from her Sony Walkman. With a cigarette in her left hand, she strummed an imaginary bass guitar with fingers that bulged at the tips. In her twenties, she'd played the real thing with the punk band Rockets Asking Forgiveness. Despite the mild weather, a knit cap covered her bald scalp. Weight loss from chemotherapy had made her even thinner so her favorite purple sweater vest hung loosely from her shoulders. A silver Celtic knot swung from a chain around her neck as she moved to the beat. When Rowan noticed Grady watching, she froze and grinned. She stubbed out her cigarette and hurried inside.

"Grady honey, I didn't see you. Want some dinner?"

"No thanks. I'll just grab some cheese and head over to the dojo."

"Nonsense! I'll grill some salmon. It'll just take a minute." Rowan handed him one of her Amnesty International petitions.

"What's this?" Grady signed his name beneath the five signatures she'd already collected.

"The Turkish government is prosecuting some publisher because he printed a book that mentioned the Armenians." She heated a frying pan on the stove, removed the salmon from the refrigerator, and peeled off the plastic wrap.

"Marisol's mom said you might want to see her acupuncturist." Grady held up the card.

Rowan glanced at it. "Add it to the pile. How's Marisol doing, anyway?"

"She's already studying for next-year's classes." Grady set the acupuncturist's card next to the get-well cards that his mom couldn't bring herself to throw away.

"Smart girl. You'd do well to follow her example." The salmon sizzled when Rowan set it in the pan.

"Has the mail come yet?" he asked.

"No, it keeps coming later and later. Last Friday the mailman didn't get here until 7:00. I called the post office and…" Rowan grew pale.

"You okay, mom?"

Rowan put a hand over her mouth and dashed to the bathroom. Grady followed and stood helplessly outside the door while she retched. The toilet flushed but Rowan didn't come out. Grady returned to the kitchen where he turned off the burner and opened the window to let the smoke out.

He choked down the overcooked fillet and drove to the aikido school. Once inside the door, he set his shoes on the rack and changed into his gi in the locker room. Still tying his belt, Grady stepped onto the mat with only moments to spare before a senior student led the class through warm-up exercises. Then Wakayama Sensei stepped into the practice area.

"Line up!"

Students kneeled in the sitting posture, called *seiza*, in a line that stretched across the practice area. As Grady felt the canvas-covered mat give slightly under his knees, a sense of well-being came over him. He glanced back and forth and positioned himself so his knees lined up with the others'. Everything in the dojo was neat, clean, and in its place from the altar with a photo of aikido's wispy-bearded founder, Morihei Ueshiba, to the weapons racks that held staffs and wooden swords. The black belts in their dark *hakama* sat to Grady's right. Having only attained the rank of third *kyu*, he sat with the lower-ranking students who wore white gis and white belts. In a karate dojo, someone with his rank would wear a brown belt but aikido avoided these trappings of status. An aikido student wears a white belt until promoted to black. Grady's black belt was still a few years off. One of Wakayama Sensei's students ran a dojo in Seattle so once Grady got accepted at the University of Washington, he could continue toward his goal without having to learn a different (and less effective) way of doing his techniques.

Wakayama Sensei bowed before stepping onto the mat, strode to his place in front of the class, and lowered his five foot five inch frame into *seiza*. He clapped his hands twice and bowed toward the altar. The students did the same. Sensei pivoted to face the class. Teacher and students bowed to one another.

"*Onegeishi masu*," Sensei said.

"*Onegeishi masu*," the class echoed.

Sensei pointed to one of the black belts who rose and rushed forward with a downward strike. Slipping to the side and behind the attacker, Sensei spun him in a half circle to the mat. The attacker sprang to his feet and tried again with the same result. After a few repetitions, Sensei stopped his demonstration and allowed the class to practice *iriminage*, the entering throw.

"*Onegeishi masu*." Grady bowed to the student on his right.

Both stood and the student attacked. Grady performed the technique and brought his opponent down but it felt a little awkward and forced. Posture! Grady straightened his back. Remembering the maxim that the difference between life and death was as small as the width of a sheet of paper, he tried to dodge so his opponent's strike just missed. With each successive repetition, he perfected his body placement and unbalanced his opponent with more grace until his motions seemed almost frictionless. Then it was his turn to attack.

That night Sensei demonstrated *iriminage* from other attacks, such as a straight punch and a diagonal strike in which he swept the attacking arm out of the way before entering. As the students mimicked his techniques, the dojo became a celebration of spinning bodies with the occasional slap of a break fall punctuating the air. The Sorry Girls, Jane and Courtney, were at it too. When their partners attacked, the ladies dropped them to the mat and murmured, "Sorry," or, "Excuse me."

Sometimes the marvel of what he was learning sent Grady into a reverie. Instead of hitting back, the aikido practitioner used his skill to maneuver his opponent into a restraint. It was the ultimate expression of nonviolence, one he wished the police and military would learn. He would have been embarrassed to admit it but Grady felt his destiny was to apply Morihei Ueshiba's method on a grander scale. He wasn't sure how, maybe with the police. The FBI's website said they were hiring agents with skills in crucial languages. If he studied Korean at college, he'd have a leg up. It would be close to Japanese and it had an alphabet so he wouldn't have to memorize all those characters. Still, he wondered if he could fit into the law enforcement culture.

Near the end of class, Sensei chose the Refrigerator, a black belt nicknamed for his mass, to demonstrate the night's final technique. The big man grasped Sensei's hands from behind. The instructor pivoted in place while raising a hand. Then he dropped his arm sending the Refrigerator to his knees.

When it was time to practice, students on both sides of Grady turned their backs on him for other partners. Grady looked back and forth like an abandoned duckling until the Refrigerator smiled and joined him. Grady tried to do the technique but the big man's grasp immobilized him like a Vice-Grip. As Grady yanked his arms to no avail, insecurities sprouted like crabgrass in his mind. Everything had been working so well before but now he had nothing. Maybe the whole thing was a fake and he'd never really get it. His face grew hot. He wanted more than anything to go hide in the changing room but the Refrigerator's grip pinned him to this place of struggle. Noting Grady's difficulty, Sensei came to help.

"Think, Grady. Even though your opponent is bigger than you, your mind is not small. Outsmart his strength by relaxing your arms and using the muscles in your hips and legs."

With Sensei's coaching Grady brought the Refrigerator to his knees. The class finished up. Grady changed and got into his old car for the drive home. After backing out of the parking spot, he shifted into drive and leaned back. His sweaty shirt stuck to the seat. Grady pulled onto Encinitas Boulevard and reflected on the night's lesson. For a while, everything had seemed hopeless but with the right technique he'd been able to triumph. Maybe all life's challenges were that way. If only he could find the book that laid it all out. "Mom's got cancer, apply *shiho nage*." Grady passed Akbar's Pizza, turned onto Elm, pulled into the driveway, and parked behind his father's Passat. Once inside the door, Grady took off his shoes and set them neatly on the entryway floor.

Earl Evans was watching CNN in the living room. William Kristol was explaining why Saddam Hussein had to go. Two empty beer bottles lay on the table within reach of the easy chair Earl occupied. The other physicists at Jupiter Labs referred to Grady's father as Mr. Peanut behind his back due to the shape his paunch gave his otherwise narrow body. Although a CEO is never popular with his minions, an independent observer would have to agree with the assessment. Even Earl's balding head, with its long thinning blonde hair, resembled the popular legume.

"Hi dad," Grady said. "Where's mom?"

"Asleep." A commercial came on and Earl clicked the remote to change the channel. "How was your class?"

"Good." Grady carried his gym bag into the alcove that opened out of the kitchen and loaded his sweaty gi into the washer. His father followed.

"Pull up a chair. Let's chat a bit."

"Okay." Grady threw a scoop of detergent into the washer and turned the dial.

Could this be it? Would his father finally buy him the practice sword he'd been asking for? Then he could really make progress as the sword is the heart of aikido technique. Grady sat across the kitchen table from his father. A blue and white Bic pen lay on the surface with its copper-colored tip pointing like an incoming arrow at Grady's belly. He swiveled his chair so a line extending from the tip would miss him. Then Grady thought better of it, reached forward, and rotated the pen ninety degrees.

"Want a beer?" Without waiting for a response, Earl took two bottles of Pacifico from the refrigerator, removed the caps, and handed one to his son. "Cheers." Earl took a seat across the kitchen table. "So, how's the car running?"

"It's okay."

"I noticed that Southwest Window Tinting has a special this week, only fifty bucks. It's over by that shopping mall with the French bakery where I got the cake for your mother's birthday. You know the one I mean?"

"Not really." Grady took a drink of his beer.

"If you go south on El Camino to where it loops into Manchester, you'll pass an apartment complex with old brick-and-white trim." Earl's voice sped up. "Then you'll want to take a left at the road across from that church. The name starts with an H, Hyacinth, High Line, something like that. Now if you get to the ARCO station, you've gone too far."

"Okay." It didn't look like a sword was in Grady's future. He looked at the clock. It was already 9:45. He needed to take a shower and get to bed.

"You remember what I told you about your mom's lung cancer?" Earl asked.

"That she was lucky because it could be treated with radiation and chemo."

"That's right," Earl said. "Radiation and chemo can knock out small cell lung cancer because it grows fast." Earl shifted in his seat. "Your mother and I talked with Dr. Singh the other day. He said that even with treatment your mother's not likely to live more than two years."

"That's it? He just said she's going to die?"

"He gave us the usual song and dance about scientific progress and how we shouldn't lose hope." Earl took a swig from the bottle. "But the upshot was two years."

"Wow." Grady didn't know what to say. He would never admit it but a sense of relief rose in him like a balloon that's string had been cut. No more hospitals! No more bills! No more uncertainty! Then guilt dragged it back to the muddy earth. How could he feel that way about his mother's death?

"This came for you, today." Earl took a folded letter written on University of Washington stationary from his pocket and set it on the table. As Grady reached for it Earl intercepted his hand. "I want you to pretend you never got this."

Grady looked from the letter to his father's eyes. He had to be kidding. Didn't he know Grady's future in the land of clean air and tall trees was riding on the letter?

"I need you to do this for your mother. Before she dies she wants us to travel around the world together as a family. She'll be a lot happier if she thinks there's nothing holding you back." Earl released the grip on Grady's hand. "Do this for me, and I'll see you get through school. You might have to take out some loans but we'll get you through school."

The phone rang. Earl shot out of his chair and snatched the receiver off the wall.

"Hello." He listened for a minute before turning to Grady. "I need to take this in the other room."

Earl walked down the hall, returned to the kitchen to hang up the phone, and went back. Grady sipped his beer while listening to his father's muffled voice coming from the home office. Earl returned a few minutes later.

"I need to go to the office for a bit. There are some last-minute snags on the SBIR that's due tomorrow." Earl put on a blue, plaid jacket that Grady hadn't seen before. "Remember what I said about the letter."

"Fine." Grady shoved the unopened envelope in his pocket.

"I might be a while so don't stay up. I'll see you in the morning. Okay?"

Grady nodded and finished his beer.

CHAPTER 2

Grady climbed the stairs to his room, tossed the gym bag in the corner, and set the buff-colored envelope on his desk. After a quick shower, he changed into a ratty pair of shorts and stared at the envelope. Should he open it? If he didn't get accepted going on the trip would be no great loss. Then he'd be a loser and his gesture to his dying mother would be meaningless. It would be better not to open it. Grady set the alarm clock. Curiosity got the better of him. He returned to the desk and tore open the envelope.

Dear Grady,
Congratulations on your acceptance to the University of Washington.
You now face the difficult task of choosing which college or university to attend. With over a hundred available majors and a faculty that includes three Nobel Prize winners, the University of Washington, we feel, offers your best choice. You'll find Seattle is one of America's most beautiful and entertaining cities. Why not come for a visit?
I look forward to seeing you.

Yours truly,
R. Davis Snelling
Admissions Chair

"Shit!"
Grady rubbed his thumb over the embossed logo on the letterhead. He was so close – Marisol, the dojo in Seattle, and Mount Rainier but how could he not go on the trip? More immediately, what would he tell Marisol? If he said that Washington had accepted him, she would be furious with him for not attending. He and Marisol had promised to always be honest. How could he go back on his word? Grady folded the letter and stashed it under his socks in a drawer. He hated his father.

Too keyed up to sleep, he carried his wooden sword out to the patio and practiced his eight-direction cuts under the harsh light as moths bumped into the bulb. With each vertical swing, he imagined slaying his oppressors. Cut – his sword smashes his father's skull.

Turn one hundred eighty degrees and cut down a doctor in a white lab coat. Turn ninety an insurance adjustor. Turn and cut down a tobacco executive. Turn, cut, turn, cut. His sword cut down the twisted cells in his mother's lungs. Casting his sword like a fishing rod, he put all his strength into his strikes until he felt a sharp tear in his elbow. Grady set the sword down and went inside to ice his hurt arm.

Grady put off telling Marisol by going to aikido on Friday night. The extra day didn't help. He still had no idea how to answer the inevitable question on Saturday. He didn't have much money so he and Marisol met at the coffee shop across from the movie theater. As usual, teen smokers, their cigarette tips glowing like malignant cherries, congregated outside. A willowy blonde girl with thick eye makeup intercepted Grady by the entrance.

"How's your mom?" she asked.

"Getting by," Grady replied.

Once inside he looked around. A group of teens with pierced lips and eyebrows sprawled on the overstuffed couch. A handful of guys typed on their laptops oblivious to the crowd. Grady spotted two free seats at a table covered with empty plates and mugs. He sent Marisol to hold their place while he ordered.

The woman behind the counter wore a short sleeveless shirt that let her tattoos show. Red, green, and blue, they swirled on her smooth, pink skin. The middle-aged couple in front of Grady had no concern for the people waiting behind them in line. They asked pointless questions and conferred about their preferences before practically buying the entire store. While waiting, Grady stole glimpses of the dimples and oak tree tattoo on the small of the counter-girl's back whenever she bent over. What would it be like to make love to a decorated woman? Marisol thought tattoos were a desecration of a woman's body. The older couple finally carried off their food. Grady ordered two green teas with a slice of carrot cake and carried them to the table.

Usually musicians played on weekends but the stage area was empty except for a microphone and impoverished tip jar. Maybe the performers were taking a break. Grady passed Marisol her tea. He would have welcomed a discussion about their least favorite teacher, Paris's street layout, or the price of chocolate in Venezuela, anything to postpone talking about his college application. He was not so lucky.

"Have you heard from Washington, yet?" Marisol asked.

"Well, the thing is…" Grady looked at the empty space behind the microphone in a silent plea to the gods to make it too noisy for conversation. "I kind of promised my folks to go on this trip." His words came faster. "I don't know if I should go. Maybe I could try to get out of it but my mom's giving up on her treatment and wants to see the world before she, you know…"

"How long will you be gone?"

"A year, I guess."

Marisol's eyes filled with sympathy. She reached across the table to take his hand. "Of course, you should go, Grady. She's your mother. It's only for a year and being apart will make our relationship stronger. There are Internet cafes all over the place and you can e-mail me about the cities you visit. I'm worried about you flying, though. What if some terrorist tries to blow up the plane?"

"Then I'll kick his ass." Grady tightened his free hand into a fist and pictured Richard Reid in his stringy hair and orange, prison jumpsuit. It would sure feel great to bust the shoe bomber's potato-shaped nose. That wasn't what the aikido philosophy taught but Grady doubted Wakayama Sensei would object.

"I'll miss you." Marisol squeezed Grady's hand and let it drop. "Maybe being alone will encourage me to get more studying done. That way, I'll be sitting pretty when you show up in Seattle next year. Have you talked to the admission office yet?"

Grady shook his head.

"I bet if you told them about your situation, they'd keep your application open. That way you wouldn't have to reapply when you get back."

"I never thought of that." Grady stroked the sparse stubble on his chin. If only there were some money left for school after the trip. Like his dad said, he could get a student loan but Grady had hoped to graduate without a $20,000 debt hanging over his head. Maybe he could work for a year. He felt his cup. The tea had cooled enough to drink without burning his tongue.

"So, have you planned the trip yet?" Marisol asked.

"Well, dad wants to keep mom away from places that are too third-world. I guess we'll start off in Europe, spend the winter in

Australia, and swing through Asia in the spring."

"You lucky bastard! Paris and Rome are great!" Marisol bounced in her chair. "I wish I were going with you."

A screech interrupted their conversation. The saxophonist, who'd come on stage, jerked the microphone away from the speaker to quiet the feedback. He wore a 1950s short-brimmed fedora over his unkempt, shoulder-length hair. Long, yellowed fingernails that curled like a Mandarin's made Grady doubt he could play his instrument. Somehow the saxophonist managed the keys and played a passable imitation of John Coltrane. Being unfamiliar with the original, Grady and Marisol listened entranced until it was time to go home.

As always on Sunday night, Grady and his parents gathered around the kitchen table for their weekly penny poker game. Ever since Rowan had discovered online Texas Hold'em, she'd insisted on this ritual to promote family unity and teach Grady "important life lessons." Grady wasn't sure what these lessons were, maybe that a flush beats a straight. Or was it the other way around? The rules were simple: no talk about cancer, no talk about jobs, and no talk about school.

Rowan upended the penny jar and the coins clattered onto the table's Formica surface. While Grady and Rowan counted a hundred pennies each from the pile, Earl got a beer from the refrigerator. Consequently mother and son had to wait while he counted out his stake. The remaining pennies went back in the jar.

Rowan shuffled and dealt everyone two cards face down. Grady lifted the edges of his hole cards off the table. He had an unsuited Queen and Five – a crummy hand. Rowan tossed two cents into the pot. As the small blind, Grady had already put in a penny. He needed to wager another to stay in the hand. Like it mattered one way or another. It wasn't even his money. Might as well make his mother happy. He pushed forward a penny.

"Raise!" Earl tossed two more cents into the pot. Bluffing was a typical strategy for him.

Rowan matched his bet. Grady folded and mucked his cards. Rowan dealt a Queen, Eight, and Three on the flop and then went on to win the hand with a pair of Eights. If Grady had called, he would have won the pot with a pair of Queens.

Grady dealt the next hand, followed by Earl. For the next few hours, Grady played a conservative game that minimized his losses. By the time they stopped at 10:00, Grady was down to seventy-nine cents and Rowan as always, was the winner. Having spectacularly flamed out an hour earlier, Earl had to put away the pennies.

Grady got out of school early on Wednesday to drive Rowan to the cancer center for her chemo. He passed a white Pontiac sedan parked out front when he pulled into the driveway. He opened the door and heard an unfamiliar voice coming from the living room.

"Naturally, I'd like to get started as soon as possible," the man said with a Brooklyn accent. "The school year ends on May 20. Could you be ready for me to move in on the 27th?"

Grady closed the front door.

"Grady," Earl called from the living room, "come meet Professor Berkowitz."

Grady stepped into the living room and found middle-aged man with a bald crown sitting on the sofa across from his father. Gray streaked the stranger's beard and remaining hair. Two beer bottles rested on the table between the two men.

"Professor Berkowitz is doing a sabbatical at the Neuroscience Institute. He's interested in renting our house." Earl took a drink.

"Your father told me you want to be a Cornhusker." The professor remained seated. "We can always use a good student at Nebraska."

"Thanks." Grady looked at his father. "Is mom ready?"

"Why don't you check upstairs?"

"Nice to meet you, Grady," the professor called as Grady climbed the stairs.

"Did you say you had a daughter, Jim?" Earl resumed his conversation with the professor. "I'll bet Grady's room will be perfect for her."

Rowan emerged from the bedroom as Grady reached the top of the stairs.

"Ready to go?" she asked.

The two bid goodbye to Earl and his guest and walked outside to Grady's beat-up Volvo. He drove south on I-5. Even at this time of day, traffic was heavy.

"You're going to need to get a passport." Rowan dug through her purse and withdrew a twenty-dollar bill, which she gave Grady. "Go to Kinko's and get two passport photos. Earl said he'd get your birth certificate out of the safe deposit box. Then we'll have to go to the Oceanside post office to put in your application. We'll also need to see about vaccinations. Remind me to check before we leave the hospital."

"Okay." Grady stuffed the money into his pants pocket.

"So how do you feel about going away for a whole year?"

The muscles tensed in Grady's shoulders like they did in trig class whenever Mr. Anderson asked him to solve a problem on the blackboard. How could he make the lie convincing? A Toyota changed lanes without signaling.

"Shit!" Grady slammed on the brakes. "Sorry mom. I guess I'm just bummed I didn't get into U Dub. Taking a year off will give me some perspective. When I get back, I can take the SATs over and maybe improve my chances."

"What about Marisol?" Rowan looked at Grady as if he were raising with a pair of Twos.

"Mom! She's got to study her ass off her first year! I'd be lucky to see her an hour a week. It's going to work out fine. Really."

"Would you like to invite her to join us this summer?" Rowan asked. "You two could go off on your own for a bit and we'd meet up when she went back. She could even come during Christmas break, too."

"Yeah." Grady stroked his chin. "I like that idea. I like it a lot."

"Want to put some music on?" Rowan asked.

"Okay." Grady reached behind the seat for the nylon CD holder, zipped it open, and shifted his eyes back and forth between its contents and the road. He flipped past Death Cab for Cutie and chose Social Distortion instead.

Grady kept the volume low. His mother didn't complain. He followed Genesee to the UCSD Thornton Hospital and found a parking spot. The new Moores Cancer Center glinted like a shard of broken glass in the sunlight. As always, Grady would shower and change clothes when he got home. He didn't want to pick up an infection from all those people with weak immune systems. He and his mother entered and navigated a series of hallways and elevators before reaching the appropriate waiting room. Grady found a pair of seats away from the other patients while his mother checked in. Careful to keep his forearms off the armrests, Grady lowered himself into a blue, cloth-covered chair.

"Why are you sitting all the way back here?" Rowan asked when she returned from the front desk. She sat down and began leafing through an old copy of *Cosmopolitan* without expecting a reply.

"Rowan," a nurse in floral scrubs called ten minutes later.

Grady's mother made her way toward the entryway that led to the treatment area. With little else to do Grady looked around the room. Not all patients had lost their hair. Some women seemed to have kept theirs but several could be wearing wigs. A bearded man in his thirties left the treatment area. An older couple, she with a gray helmet of sprayed hair and he with a Ronald Reagan pompadour, made their way from the check in to their seats. The man wore a red plaid shirt over his barrel-shaped torso and baggy jeans over spindly legs. After they sat down, his wife rested her hand on his forearm.

A teenaged woman took a seat a few chairs away from Grady. She wore the typical Goth getup: black clothes, pale makeup, black lipstick, and flaking black nail polish. The only deviation was the black scarf over her bald head. Sick people were bad enough but nothing was more depressing than a Goth at a cancer clinic. As if reading Grady's mind, she turned her large blue eyes toward him. Grady quickly looked away. The afterimage of clotted blood on her cracked lips burned in his mind. He opened the magazine his mother had set down to cover up his unease.

"Read *Cosmo* much?" the woman asked.

"Oh, it's my mother's." Grady's face grew hot. "She's in back." He set the *Cosmopolitan* down and scanned the room for a more suitable magazine.

"What's her diagnosis?"

"Lung."

"Hmm, that's too bad. I'm a Hodgkin's, myself."

"Oh." Grady got up and walked to the magazine rack near the check-in desk. Hodgkin's! That was all right. He'd heard most patients survive. Grady sorted through the two-year-old issues of *People* and *Woman's Day* before finding a copy of *Popular Mechanics* and returning to his chair.

The Goth girl moved closer.

"You want to go smoke a joint?" she asked. "It's legal for me."

"Oh, uh. I have to wait for my mom." Grady tried to occupy himself with an article on hydrogen-powered cars even though he'd never been interested in them before.

"Helen!" the nurse called.

"Guess I'll see you around." The Goth girl picked up her purse and went for her treatment.

"So, how are your veins, today?" the nurse asked as she escorted the Goth girl into the back room.

Patients went in. Patients came out. Grady read the magazine. He abandoned the article after a few pages and turned to one on home entertainment centers. An old woman wearing tights the color of her ashen skin hobbled out of the treatment area. Each step she took was not much longer than her foot. Grady flipped the pages and stopped at a picture of a Zodiac rigid inflatable boat.

"Let's go." Rowan placed a hand on Grady's shoulder.

He hadn't seen his mother approach.

"Do you want to check out the travel shots?" he asked.

Rowan shook her head. She walked to the car as if she were a light bulb and any sudden movement would rupture her fragile skin and spill her insides. Grady drove like an old man to avoid shattering her.

The following day Marisol got together with her girlfriends so Grady went home after school. His mother's Prius was in the driveway but his father's car wasn't there. Grady entered through the front door and dropped his backpack near the kitchen table.

"I'm home!"

No one answered. Grady tiptoed up the stairs. The door to his parents' bedroom was closed. He returned to the kitchen, got a soda, and spread his trig book, calculator, and notebook on the table. If he could get his homework done in an hour, he'd have time to kick back before heading to the dojo. When he was halfway through the second problem, the doorbell rang.

"I'm Barbara and this is Jean. We're from the First Calvary Chapel on Hudson," said the taller of the two women standing on the doorstep. Both wore modest clothes and had neatly combed hair. "And you must be Grady. It's been five or six years since we've seen you. My, how you've grown! Is your mother here?"

"She's resting now."

"How is Rowan?" Barbara leaned forward. "Is she doing okay?"

"Well, the chemotherapy's no fun," Grady said.

"We brought you some food." Jean, the shorter woman, held out a plastic bag. "There's Barbara's Swedish meatballs, potato salad, and Mrs. Anderson's famous coconut caramel bars."

"Thanks." Grady took the bag and looked inside.

"Well, we'd better be going," Barbara said. "You think we'll see you at church this Sunday?"

There it was! The fishhook in the Swedish meatballs! Grady looked at the women's expectant faces. Why couldn't these Christians ever do something nice without there being a catch?

"It depends on how my mom feels," he said.

"Tell her we're praying for her," Jean said.

"Right. Thanks for stopping by." Grady closed the door.

"Who was that?" Rowan asked. Dressed in her pale-blue robe, she'd come down the stairs while Grady had been talking to the visitors.

"Two women from the Calvary Chapel." Grady held up the plastic bag. "They brought Swedish meatballs."

"What else did they want?" Rowan leaned on the railing by the stairs.

"They wanted to know when we'd come to their church."

"I'm not even dead and the vultures are already circling," Rowan shook her head and began climbing the stairs to her room.

Earl called a family meeting and picked up a pizza on his way home from work Friday night. It was supposed to start at 6:00 but Earl was late. He took a quick shower and joined the others in the kitchen.

"Sausage and mushroom – an S &M pizza. Get it?" Earl winked at Grady.

Rowan pulled a dishtowel off the kitchen faucet and flogged her husband's bottom. Earl danced out of range and set the white, pizza box on the table. Grady lifted the cover and the smell of roasted garlic filled the roam. Realizing his error, he glanced at his mother. She didn't appear nauseous so he turned back to dinner. The pie glistened with olive oil. Cheese stretched like telephone lines as he lifted two slices onto a paper plate. He carried it into the living room, sat with a squeak on the leather couch, and slid the cheese off his pizza with a plastic fork.

When everyone had assembled, Earl switched off the TV.

"I've got some great news," he said. "Professor Berkowitz has agreed to rent the house."

"That's wonderful!" Rowan said. She sat next to Grady and held her plate demurely in her lap.

"The professor wants to move in May 27," Earl said. "How attached are you to your graduation ceremony, Grady?"

Grady bit his pizza and burned his tongue.

"Don't even think it, Earl!" Rowan said. "I'm not about to miss my son's high school graduation."

"All right. I was just asking the boy." Earl sat back in his easy chair. "I suppose we can stay in a motel for a few weeks."

"Did you get the passport photos, Grady?" Rowan asked.

Grady swallowed a mouthful. "They're in my room. Want me to get them?"

"Not now but we'd better go to the post office first thing tomorrow."

"Do you think we should do Europe or Asia first?" Earl asked. "If we did Asia, Grady would have a chance to do his karate sooner."

"It's aikido, Earl," Rowan said.

"Aikido, karate…" Earl rolled his eyes.

"Starting in Europe will be less of a culture shock. I really want to see the European museums, the Louvre, the Prado," Rowan said. "And besides there must be aikido classes in Europe."

"Any objections?" Earl looked at Grady.

"I guess not just so long as we stay out of the Mid East."

"I hear you. It's settled. We'll start in Europe." Earl clapped his hands to his thighs and sat up. "Now, there's just one more matter."

Here it comes, Grady thought.

"Professor Berkowitz doesn't want to keep your old Volvo around, Grady. Your mother and I think it would be best to sell it."

Grady set down his plate.

"We could put it in storage, of course but that would cost more than the car's worth," Earl said.

"It's your car, Grady. You can keep the money you get from selling it and get another when you get back," Rowan added.

Grady pushed the plate away from him. There was no use arguing. He'd just get the lecture he'd heard a thousand times before. "We all need to sacrifice to help your mother, blah, blah, blah."

"Fine." Grady stood. "Anything else?"

"We don't have too much time," Earl said, "so we'd better get an ad in the paper right away."

Newspaper! Grady stared at his father. Nobody put ads in newspapers anymore but Grady wasn't about to hasten the demise of his car by telling his dad about Craigslist.

CHAPTER 3

A week after the ad appeared in the *Union Tribune*, a surfer bought the Volvo for $600. The following morning the alarm clock buzzed a half-hour early. Like a zombie Grady ate his customary breakfast of fruit and oatmeal before dragging himself to the bus stop where he kept his distance from the waiting freshmen. "Oh my Gods," spiced the girls' conversations. The boys made sound effects of machine guns, explosions, and racing cars. A yellow school bus pulled up, its door yawned open, and Grady boarded with the others.

"You mind if I sit here?" One of the freshmen gestured to the empty spot next to the seat Grady had taken. Rubber bands connected the braces on the boy's upper and lower jaws, and his part wandered like the Amazon over his scalp.

Grady shrugged.

"Do you like the Left Behind series?" the freshman asked seconds after sitting.

"No." Grady opened a book and turned his back.

A wad of paper bounced off the freshman's head. He looked around but couldn't find the culprit. Fearing his neighbor's geekiness would rub off, Grady slouched to make himself a smaller target. He had three more weeks of this.

Grady tried to get rides with Marisol whenever he could. Failing that, he sat with some Chicano sophomores who were okay. Weeks passed. One Thursday in May Grady finished the last problem on his trig test. He had twenty minutes before the period ended but he'd rather drink battery acid than go over those problems again. He placed the exam on Mr. Anderson's desk, collected his books and backpack, and left the building. The June gloom had settled over Encinitas early, making the sky as gray as Grady's mood. He scanned the parking lot for Marisol's Saturn but didn't see it. He'd have to spend an hour and a half twiddling his thumbs in study hall before catching the bus home. Either that or he could walk. Grady sighed. Skip Burlow pulled his silver Miata to the curb.

"Hey Grady, what happened to your wheels?" The former quarterback had the top down in spite of the dismal weather.

"Had to sell it."

"That sucks." Skip reached across the passenger seat and opened the door. "Hop in. I'll give you a ride."

"Nice car." Grady slid into the tan leather seat and placed his backpack on the floor, holding it between his knees.

"Yeah, my parents bought it for me as a graduation/going off to USC gift." Skip shifted into gear. A gold chain hung on his wrist like a pendulum of privilege. "Your place is over on Powell, right?"

"Yeah, just past Akbar's Pizza."

As soon as they left the lot, Skip stomped the gas pedal. The engine hummed and brought the little car up to sixty in a few seconds.

"I'll sure be glad when this high school shit is over." Skip ran a hand through his dark hair.

"Don't you know these are supposed to be the best years of your life?" Grady said.

"Shoot me now." Skip maneuvered around an SUV and gestured with his middle finger at the driver. He stopped at a light and turned to Grady. "You hang around with Marisol Ortiz a lot. She seems pretty decent."

"Yeah, studies too much, though."

"Be grateful. All my girlfriends do is drink and complain." The light changed and Skip shot through the intersection. "Gets real old after a while. Hey, what are you two doing graduation night?"

"Don't know yet."

"Me and some friends are renting a few rooms at the Hotel Del. We're trying for a real class evening, no juvenile asshole stuff. Maybe you two would like to come."

"Sounds great!" Grady said.

They drove past Akbar's Pizza.

"I had your mom for French 101 before she got sick," Skip said. "Must be tough on her with the cancer and all. She in a lot of pain?"

"At times," Grady said.

"You think you could get me some of her Oxy?" Skip asked.

Grady pictured the tan prescription bottles lining the medicine cabinet. All he'd have to do was slip a few capsules in his pocket. His mother would never miss them. He looked at Skip who'd always looked cooler and more grownup than his classmates. Fuck him!

"Her doctor's kind of lame." Grady focused on Skip's eyes. "He never prescribed any of that stuff."

"Too bad."

Grady gave directions and soon Skip pulled to Grady's driveway.

"Let me know about the party," Skip said.

"Sure thing." Grady climbed out of the bucket seat. "Thanks for the ride." He knew he'd never hear from Skip again.

The violet carry-on bag lay open on Grady's bed. He'd wanted a backpack like the ones sold at Vans but Rowan had insisted on three identical upright rolling bags. The goofy color supposedly would make them easy to spot on a luggage carousel. It was Grady's last night in their home and he was packing for the upcoming trip.

What would he take to last a whole year? Wakayama Sensei had told of how Buddhist monks live with only two robes and a set of bowls. Grady doubted he could get by with that little but he'd try to travel light. His school supplies were in a cardboard box by the door. He'd take them to the hotel and then abandon them after graduation. With that settled he only had to decide what to take on the trip.

Grady placed his passport and the six hundred dollars he'd gotten for his car in his new money belt and zipped that in an external pocket. For toiletries he placed a toothbrush, nail clippers, and razor in a Ziplock bag. He could do without deodorant and wash his hair with bar soap. Grady could count on his mother for sunscreen and over-the-counter medicines. She was a walking drugstore. He packed his camou pants, a pair of dark slacks, two dress shirts, three polo shirts, three T-shirts including his worn Anarchy in the UK, socks, underwear, his Death or Glory hooded sweatshirt, and a plastic poncho in case it rained.

What else did he need? He tried to fit two gis but only had room for one. He could wear his Vans Old Skool sneakers but he tossed in a pair of cloth Kung Fu shoes as a backup. They were light. He added a hair brush, swimming trunks, sunglasses, Japanese and European phrasebooks, more Ziplock bags, and a garbage bag to segregate dirty clothes.

Grady zipped the bag closed. It was all he'd need for a whole year. His eyes drifted to the closet. Should he take a tie? Fuck it! If any restaurants required a tie, he wouldn't go.

The following morning the professor took possession of the Evans's house. Grady waited with his mother in her Toyota Prius while Earl turned over the keys. From the passenger's side Grady took a last look at the house that had been his home for the past fifteen years. The carport's support was still worn where he'd taped a rubber pad to make a karate striking post he'd never used. He stared at the porch and remembered how he'd tumbled off it on a skateboard and broken his wrist. Then there was the sooty mark on the stucco where he and a friend had set off an M-80 and caught the grass on fire. His parents had never found out about that one.

Earl shook the professor's hand and came to the Prius's window. "It's the Hideaway over by the Poinsettia exit. I'll lead the way."

They followed Earl's Passat onto the Interstate, keeping the yellow, Support Our Troops sticker on his bumper in view. After a fifteen-minute drive they arrived at the motel. Earl checked in at the front desk and returned with two keys.

"They didn't have adjoining rooms so they put Grady across the courtyard in 210." Earl handed Grady a key. "After you get settled, you want to go to lunch, maybe in a half hour?"

"Actually, I kind of want to go to aikido." Grady looked at his watch. The class started in an hour. "Mind if I borrow your car?"

"Sure, we're in 129. Come by when you're ready."

Grady wheeled his luggage past the deserted swimming pool. A few leaves floated on the water and many deck chairs had missing webbing. When he hauled his bag up the worn concrete steps, the elbow he'd injured weeks earlier began to hurt so he switched his bag to the other hand. His arm would get better in time. It had to because he wasn't going to let the doctors turn him into an invalid like his mother. Grady circled the walkway and found his room. The inside smelled of disinfectant, which was better than stale cigarette smoke in his opinion. He tossed his bag on the bed and stared at the painting of a cowboy and covered wagon on the wall. It sure seemed sterile. Grady turned on the TV to mask the traffic sounds coming from the freeway. He flipped the channels. He'd already seen the movie on HBO so he watched music videos until he was ready to leave.

At empty-hand class that afternoon Sensei Wakayama taught defenses from a straight punch. He began with an evasion, turned under his opponent's arm, and ended up with a wristlock called *sankyo*. When it was time to choose partners Grady noted Sensitive Dan, sitting to his right, and chose the partner on his left to avoid him. Sensitive Dan had earned his nickname through application of brute force techniques. A slight, quiet man with blonde highlights in his hair, Sensitive Dan didn't give the appearance of aggression but Sensei's inner megalomaniac theory held that like sharks small guys were always the most aggressive.

Whenever it was time to sit and watch Sensei demonstrate, Grady placed himself so he had a buffer of other students between himself and Sensitive Dan but eventually Dan caught up with him. The technique was *kote gaeshi*, a slip to the outside of the punch and bend of the wrist that forced the attacker into a mild backward fall much like sitting. Grady had little trouble defeating Dan's punches. This didn't stop Dan from correcting him. Ever since Dan had been promoted to second *kyu*, he'd acted like a know it all. The man understood nothing about aikido but got away with shoddy techniques by using muscle and momentum. Grady nodded and then it was his turn to attack. Rather than stepping to the outside, Dan stepped inside the punch, pivoted, and twisted Grady's wrist to the side. Pain shot through Grady's arm. The technique offered him two choices: a broken wrist or jumping over the arm to land hard on the mat in a break fall, a prospect Grady regarded with terror. He'd mastered the gentle rolls common for most aikido techniques but had yet to learn break falls. Somehow Grady managed to turn out of Dan's wristlock and land unglamorously on his tailbone.

"I'm going to take a rest." Grady bowed to Sensitive Dan and got off the mat.

Fuming he walked down the hall toward the water fountain. The sound of feet thumping to the recorded theme from "Fame" came from inside the dance studio. At the fountain Grady pushed the button and let the water run. The nerve of that man! Just because he could go to a seminar and get promoted! Well, Grady could have gone too if his mother hadn't had cancer! Somebody ought to do something about him! Grady paused. This train of thought wasn't very aiki. He took a mouthful of tepid water and returned to the mat.

Grady stayed for the weapons class. He'd left his staff and wooden sword at the house so he had to use one of the spindly swords from the rack on the dojo's wall. Sensei Wakayama went over the twelve paired sword drills. Things went well for Grady until he partnered once more with Sensitive Dan. During that practice session Grady stepped to the inside and held his sword low to block Dan's diagonal slash at his knee. Sounding like a rifle shot, the cheap dojo sword cracked as Dan powered through. Sensei's face grew red.

"Sorry, Sensei." Grady held up the broken sword.

Sensei Wakayama looked from Grady to Dan and back again before chuckling. He retrieved a *subarito*, a thick wooden sword resembling an oar that was used to build muscle, and handed it to Grady. Everyone laughed.

After class a number of students had lunch at Akbar's Pizza. It began life as a fish-and-chips outlet. Its new Pakistani owners saw no need to change décor with the new cuisine. After 9-11 some vandals broke a few of their windows. Rowan helped organize a demonstration in support of the owners and Grady convinced members of the dojo to come. They'd been eating there ever since. Grady and the Refrigerator commandeered a few tables by the fish net on the wall. Sensei arrived followed by several students. As usual Carl the Navigator got lost.

"So, Sensitive Dan struck again," the Refrigerator said with a maniacal laugh.

"There ought to be some kind of special insurance to cover all the swords he breaks," a junior black belt said.

"Wouldn't work." The Refrigerator sipped his beer. "Insurance companies would go bankrupt."

"Did I ever tell you about Sensitive Dan at the police defensive tactics seminar?" a student asked.

"I've got a Sensitive Dan story," the Refrigerator said. "We were at the aikido summer camp in Steamboat and Dan was staying in his tent. I warned him about food and bears but of course he didn't listen. When we returned from an afternoon session, there's this black bear sticking his nose in Dan's tent. A normal man would give a hungry animal with three-inch claws a wide berth but Sensitive Dan drew his *bokken* and charged. The bear ran away, too."

The laughter ceased when Sensitive Dan walked in the door.

"What's going on?" he asked when he sat at the table.

"I was just talking about the Systema seminar I went to in Las Vegas," the Refrigerator said.

"That's that Russian art. Isn't it?"

"Yeah, it's really cool." The Refrigerator launched into a description of the techniques he'd learned.

The pizzas came. As usual Grady removed the cheese and topping from his slices. He didn't need all that fat. After an hour of banter Grady decided he'd better return his father's car.

"Before you go, here's a little something for you." Sensei Wakayama gave Grady a package.

Grady peeled the wrapping paper from a book titled *Aikido in Everyday Life*.

"The real purpose of aikido is to bring peace outside the dojo," Sensei said. "Terry Dobson was one of the few Westerners to train with O Sensei. He tried to apply the principle of blending to conflicts with coworkers and others. I attended some of his seminars, before he died. He was a really great guy."

"Thank you, Sensei."

"See you, Grady," everyone chimed when Grady walked out the door.

Grady looked at the book as soon as he got back to the motel. He was enthralled almost immediately after getting past the cover that showed a *hakama*-clad woman in a dojo. All his life he'd been searching for a way to deal with jerks without screaming his head off or getting walked on. This was it! The author broke responses down into triangles, squares, and circles. Depending on its orientation a triangle could be either a counterattack or a retreat. A square represented doing nothing, useful when you need more time. And a circle could represent bargaining, deceit, or an aiki response of empathizing with your attacker and then changing his direction. Grady found a pad of paper and started scribbling notes. He made it through chapter five before Marisol called and asked what he was doing for dinner.

On the night of the prom Grady stood before the mirror. The jacket was tight around his shoulders and the sleeves hiked up whenever he extended his arms. Oh well, that's what he got for renting a tuxedo at the last minute – black jacket and pants, a pair of uncomfortable patent leather shoes, and a cummerbund he didn't know what to do with. Grady checked his bow tie in the mirror and stepped out of the bathroom.

"Let me help you with that." Earl motioned for Grady to take off his jacket and tied the cummerbund around his son's waist. "There you go."

Grady put on the jacket and checked that the forty-dollar tickets were still in the pocket.

"You have enough money?" Earl asked.

"I think so."

"Take a little extra." Earl took out his wallet and handed over a half-dozen twenties along with the keys to his Passat. "Let's go show your mother."

"Grady, you look so handsome." Rowan straightened Grady's tie and brushed a hair off his shoulder. "You'd better not keep your date waiting. I'll walk you to the car."

Rowan grabbed her purse and escorted Grady to the parking lot. The two paused beside the Passat.

"Do you have enough money?"

"Yes, mom."

"Here." She opened her purse and gave Grady a hundred dollars. "Take this just in case." Rowan paused, removed a box of condoms, and handed these to Grady. "Take these too."

"Mom, I…"

Rowan raised a hand to silence his protest. "Just promise you'll use them if the need arises."

"Okay, mom."

The Evans were never a physically demonstrative family but that night before sending him on his big step toward adulthood Rowan hugged her son as tightly as a drowning woman holds a life preserver. Marisol was waiting when Grady arrived at her house. She'd chosen a sequined, white dress that showed off her womanly figure and highlighted her tanned arms and shoulders.

The waiter at Le Jardin showed them to their table and held Marisol's chair while she sat. Each place at the table had a dinner plate, appetizer plate, two forks, two spoons, a butter knife, two glasses, and a coffee cup. Sitting across from the massive array of cutlery made it impossible for Grady to twist his body so none of the points aimed at him. There was no logical reason for this to cause a personal misfortune. Still, a sense of unease lingered like a wolf outside the light of a campfire. So much could go wrong with his life: AIDS, an unwanted pregnancy, and cancer, for example. He could somehow end up in prison. Only the naive believed their lives would be happy. Grady examined the menu and almost choked at the prices. For him a salad was a salad and nothing justified these costs. But he ordered one anyway because eating at expensive French restaurants was what you did as a grownup. He and Marisol enjoyed their meals. The scallops in wine sauce were delicious although the portions were small, and the Peach Melba was outstanding. Even with two hundred dollars in his pocket, Grady felt as if he were stepping into the uncharted territory of adulthood when the bill came. How would he ever earn enough money to afford this kind of thing in the future? Grady paid and added a twenty-percent tip.

"Thank you, sir," said the waiter as Grady escorted Marisol out the door.

Entering adulthood frightened Grady but he'd soon learn that returning to childhood would be worse. The school had rented the Pines Hotel's ballroom in Del Mar for the prom. Grady paid ten dollars to park in the lot and joined the swarm of students in formal wear heading toward the entrance.

"Hey Grady!" Warren Goodman slapped him on the back. "Want a snort?" Warren, who was joining the Marines after graduation, removed a silver flask from his jacket pocket.

Grady took a sip to be polite. Whatever Warren had in there burned like rocket fuel. He held out the flask to Marisol who shook her head. A sign in the lobby directed students to the Cambden Ballroom but anyone could have found the prom by following the sound of recorded music. In the hallway leading to the ballroom a dozen young women in pastel dresses leaned against the wall by the ladies room.

"Underwear check," murmured one as Grady and Marisol passed.

A brunette, her face flushed in embarrassment, exited. "Come on," she latched onto the arm of a boy in a sky blue jacket. "I have to go home and change."

Grady presented his tickets to Mrs. Johnson at the ballroom's entrance.

"If you'll just join the line of girls by the door, dear," she said to Marisol.

"What's that all about?"

"We need to make sure no one's wearing thongs tonight, dear."

Marisol formed her mouth into a slit and narrowed her eyes.

"There were some instances of lewd dancing last year," Mrs. Johnson said. "I'm afraid I can't let you in if you don't submit to the check."

"Let's get out of here," Marisol said to Grady.

"How about giving me my money back?" Grady asked Mrs. Johnson.

The plump woman folded her arms over her chest and shook her head. Grady never loved Marisol more than when the passed the women, lined up like cattle waiting for the stun gun, on the way out.

"Can you believe that shit?" Marisol screamed once they were outside.

"Fucking assholes!" Grady shook his head.

The passed a smirking parking attendant, got in the car, and sat.

"Sorry about the cost of the tickets, Grady." Marisol placed a hand on his forearm. "What do you want to do, now?"

"Screw 'em. They're not going to ruin our evening. Let's go to SOMA."

They headed south and drove around under the I-8 overpass searching for a parking spot close to the all-ages club. Despite his misgivings about wearing a tuxedo to a punk rock show, Grady and Marisol danced to exhaustion to the music of Pamela's Wetsuit, The Dan Rather Experience, and The Rejuvenators.

A knock woke Grady. He looked around in the unfamiliar darkness. This wasn't his room. Then he remembered he was in a motel. He sat up and rubbed his face. The knocking continued.

"Coming." Grady stepped into his pants, opened the door, and squinted in the bright sunshine.

"How was the prom?" Earl asked.

Grady blinked a few times. In the second it took to focus he decided his father had more important things to deal with than the underwear check that had ruined the prom. "It was okay," he said.

"When did you get in?"

"Around two."

"Yeah, I remember my prom night." A cloud of memory cast a shadow of wistfulness over Earl's features. "One of the best nights of my life." Then he was all business. "I need to drop off the Passat. Will you follow in the Prius and give me a ride back?"

"Sure."

Grady dressed and they left. He followed his father north on the Coast Highway. Even though the ocean was flat, several surfers sat on boards in the waters by the Encina power plant. Earl turned onto 78 and eventually pulled into the driveway of a yellow, wood house in Vista. Grady got out of the Prius and followed his father to the door. A stocky man whose beer belly gave him a sway back, answered. Hair oil held his gray locks in place.

"Hello, Steve. I brought the car," Earl said. "This is my son Grady."

"Come in." Steve escorted them into a kitchen that smelled of cooked cabbage. "Care for a soda?" Without waiting for a reply he dropped ice cubes into three glasses and set a gallon bottle of cola on the table.

Grady and Earl drank while Steve went outside to look at the car. He returned a few minutes later.

"I have the title right here." Earl took the document from his breast pocket.

"Let me get your check." Steve left the room, returned with a cashier's check, and gave it to Earl.

"We agreed on nine thousand dollars," Earl set the check on the table.

"Well, the thing of it is I'm a bit short until the fifteenth. If I take a distribution before then the penalties will kill me. I should be able to get you the rest in a few weeks."

"Let's go, Grady." Earl stood.

"Hold on. Hold on." Steve waved his plump hands. "How about I write you a postdated check for the balance?"

"I'll take cash," Earl said.

Steve huffed and stomped out of the room. When he returned he laid down ten hundred-dollar bills. "I hope you realize Betsy will have to do without her medicine this month because of you!"

"Pleasure doing business with you." Earl signed over the title and left the keys on the table. He scooped up the cash and check.

When they got back to the Prius Grady asked. "Do you suppose Betsy is his cow?"

"They'll cheat you any chance they get." Earl sighed. "Breaks my heart to think of that bastard driving my Passat. God, I loved that car!"

"Why didn't you sell the Prius instead?"

Earl glared at Grady as if he were the stupidest person alive. "I don't want your mother thinking we're not expecting her to come back from the trip."

Flushed with embarrassment Grady drove his father back to the motel in silence.

Grady's final weeks in high school passed faster than a Lamborghini driven by a type-A CEO. Most of it was uneventful except for the Victoria's Secret catalog he left on Mrs. Johnson's windshield. The finish of her green Honda Accord cried out for the kiss of his keys but he restrained himself from gouging the paint. No sense screwing up his graduation. Living out of a suitcase got to be a drag. He'd put up with having only a half-dozen shirts and one gi for about a week before getting more clothes from the house. He wouldn't be able to take them on the trip but in the interim it was more convenient than washing shirts every few days. He tried to get in as many aikido classes as he could but it was hard because of the car situation. Before he knew it he was standing in a crimson cap and gown in the gymnasium with his classmates. After a few cliché-ridden speeches, a walk to the podium, and a flip of the tassel on his mortarboard; life as he'd known it was over. Earl beamed and Rowan cried but for Grady graduation was anticlimactic. Marisol's grandmother had flown into town so Grady didn't get to spend much time with his girlfriend that night.

The following day, Grady's last before he left, Marisol knocked on his motel room door at 9:00 AM. She wore a light blue cotton pullover and a white skirt over bare legs. He took a moment to look at her. Now that they would soon be apart she seemed even more vibrant and precious.

"Put a decent shirt on. I'm taking you to breakfast," she said.

"Don't I get a hug first?" Grady wrapped her in his arms.

Marisol pressed into him. Grady felt the muscle under her body's façade of softness and the grind of her pubic bone. He buried his face in her hair, breathed in, and recoiled from the sour stench of stale cigarettes.

"Have you been smoking?" he asked.

"No."

"Don't lie to me. I can smell it on your hair."

"It was just one cigarette, Grady." She stepped toward the orange chair. "I didn't tell you 'cause I knew you'd overreact."

"Overreact!" Grady raised his hands. "Jesus!" His hands dropped slapping against his thighs. "How could you smoke after seeing what it did to my mom? I don't believe this!"

Marisol turned toward him. "Do you really want to spend our last day together like this?"

"I guess not."

Grady zipped open his suitcase and sorted through the folded shirts. How could somebody who'd seemed so right be so stupid? He pulled out a pale-yellow polo shirt to go with his gray camou pants and silver chain that attached his wallet to his belt loop.

They left. Outside the overcast had already burned off, unusual for that time of year. The air was still and sweet. A few children splashed each other in the pool. Marisol put her arm around Grady's waist, escorted him to her Saturn, and unlocked his door before getting behind the wheel. They drove along the coast and passed the golden-domed yoga center at Swami's. A squadron of pelicans, looking like an ill-advised aeronautical experiment gone horribly wrong, flew overhead.

"Do you remember the first time you kissed me?" Marisol asked.

"Behind the bleachers at the dance."

"Maggie Cathcart said Doug Peterson put you up to it."

"It's true." Grady looked out the window. A swell rose from the ocean's glassy surface and two surfers paddled to keep up. "But he only dared me because I told him I thought you were hot."

"Why did you think that?" Marisol asked.

"It must have been the time you wore your bedroom slippers to homeroom when you were late, the ones that look like bunnies."

"Mrs. Esposito sent me home."

"I know."

Marisol turned into the parking lot of a Mexican restaurant.

"I still have those slippers," she said.

"I know."

The restaurant was crowded but they managed to get a table by the window. Grady could see a bit of ocean through the gaps in the palm trees across the highway. He ordered eggs. When they came he punctured the yolks so the golden center ran all over the plate and mopped them up with pillowy flour tortillas. He left the fatty, refried beans mostly uneaten. Marisol picked at her yogurt and fruit and discussed her plans for a summer job.

"It depends on how much I earn," she said, "but I think joining you in Europe for a week will be okay. Where will you be in August?"

"We're starting in Ireland and going east. Maybe Italy or Greece by then."

"Oh, I'd love to see the Parthenon. School starts in mid-

September so I'd have to be back here by Labor Day. You do want me to come. Don't you?"

"Of course."

"You about done?" Marisol nodded to the waiter who brought the bill.

"You mind stopping so I can pick up some Andre the Giant stickers?" Grady asked.

"Some what?" Marisol put some money on the table.

"You know, those stickers with the creepy face that say obey. It'll be cool to post them all over the world."

"Whatever." Marisol sighed.

They decided to spend the day at Balboa Park. After stopping at a bookstore for the OBEY Giant stickers they drove to the park passing under the Cabrillo Bridge, one of Grady's favorite views. It stood like a row of white M's connecting one tree-lined canyon wall with the other. Marisol parked and they walked past the Organ Pavilion and Japanese Friendship Garden.

"Do you think our relationship can last with us being apart for a year?" she asked.

Grady chose his words as he would if he were on the witness stand. "It might be difficult but you want to concentrate on school. Remember?"

"'Cause we could agree to date other people," Marisol said.

The circuits in Grady's brain went into overdrive tallying the calculus of self-interest. Being cooped up with his parents for a year, he wouldn't have many opportunities with the opposite sex but Marisol would have plenty at college. Did he really love her enough to hold on for a year or was she only a convenience close at hand? He didn't know the answer.

"Let's see how we feel when you come out in August," he said.

They strolled along the Prado with its Spanish Colonial buildings and vendor stands along the edge of the walkway. A shirtless man with a headdress of feathers set up a boom box and did an Aztec dance to recorded Mexican music.

"Look!" Grady pointed. "The model train museum! Can we go to the model train museum?"

Marisol rolled her eyes but had to concede since it was Grady's last day. They went inside. At the ticket window she motioned Grady to put away his wallet. This day was her treat.

"Wow!" Grady hurried to the exhibits leaving her behind.

HO trains ran through mountainous miniature landscapes complete with trees, grass, and gravel track beds. Grady followed the yellow, tandem Union Pacific locomotives as they pulled their cargo of plastic freight cars past the green-roofed station and railroad crossing where a 1950s vintage auto waited on the road. Everything looked so real. There were boulders, fence posts, signal lights, telephone poles, and even water tanks for steam locomotive. Grady hovered like some all-seeing, all-powerful being. Life on the HO-scale was so much easier to control. The train turned a corner and disappeared into a tunnel only to emerge in a desert landscape and cross a trestle spanning a deep gorge.

Grady felt Marisol's arm slip around his waist. He hadn't heard her approach. Together they examined the other exhibits. After an hour she asked, "You ready to go?"

Outside they walked to where a dozen more vendors' stands circled a fountain like Conestoga wagons awaiting an Indian attack.

"Let's get our fortunes told." Marisol took Grady's hand and dragged him toward a banner depicting a red palm.

"I don't think it's such a good idea." Grady started to pull away.

"Oh, come on. It'll be fun."

Grady looked at the heavyset woman, with a hairstyle that could have come from a 1950s sitcom, who sat behind the table under the banner. What could he do if his future contained more sorrow like his mother's illness? It was better not to know.

"I don't want to do it." He stared walking away.

"Grady!" Marisol caught up with him and took his arm. "We don't have to. I thought you might like it. That's all."

The city cooperated with Marisol's plan to make Grady's last day special. Even the notorious traffic was light. After spending the afternoon at the park they ate dinner and saw a movie in Hillcrest and then drove back to Encinitas to watch the sunset from Moonlight Beach.

They sat behind a large piece of driftwood, out of sight of the crowd. The rhythmic sound of waves breaking on the sand muted the talk of the other beachgoers. Grady felt the warmth radiating from Marisol's body against his skin. He put his arm around her waist and drew her closer. She turned and offered him her soft lips. Grady's fee hand caressed her side and came to rest on her bud-like breast.

Marisol placed a warm hand on top of his to keep it there.

"Yeah, fuckin' A," a voice called from the distance. Someone laughed.

Grady withdrew his hand and Marisol straightened her clothes. Two blonde surfers, in wetsuits, carried their short boards past. Grady let them pass before kissing Marisol again. They alternated between passion and interruption until the sun was an orange crescent on a field of blue. Grady watched it inch lower. The moment the sun vanished below the horizon he saw a green circle, not much larger than the sun, with a dark dot in its center. Laughs and hoots came from people by the volleyball net.

"The green flash!" he said. "I can't believe it. I finally saw the green flash."

The temperature dropped. Grady and Marisol huddled together in the chill for a half hour before he said, "I suppose we should get going."

He took a last look at the ocean as they walked up the beach. Marisol drove him to the motel and escorted him past the empty swimming pool, up the stairs where a Ho Chi Minh trail of ants crawled along the support beam, and into his room. The clock on the nightstand said 9:20.

"I don't have to go yet." Marisol sat on the bed.

Grady kissed her. They had little time to waste on preliminaries. Rather than engaging in the usual piecemeal undressing, Marisol stood and bared herself. She came to him not as a ghostly figure of longing in his imagination but naked and real with a few pink pimples scattered on her butt, razor stubble on her ankles, and the indentations the elastic of her bra and panties had left on her torso. It frightened him a little. He stripped off his shirt and pants and then paused before shimmying out of his white briefs. Marisol got into bed while Grady rolled on one of the condoms his mother had given him on prom night. Marisol lifted the sheet and he crawled underneath the covers and into the cozy comfort of her warm flesh.

After making love Grady fell into a narcotic sleep. Several times that night he woke fearing she was gone but Marisol was always there to offer a soft shoulder for him to rest his head on. The scent of her skin soothed him. Around 4:00 AM he drifted off to sleep. They woke to the sound of birds in the early morning.

"I'd better get going." Marisol slipped on her panties and stood.

Grady watched her dress in the light from the edges of the curtains. He stepped into his pants and walked her to the door.

"I guess this is it." Marisol squeezed him for the last time. "Write me." She slipped out the door and was gone.

CHAPTER 4

Grady, Rowan, and Earl arrived at Dublin Airport in the early morning. As soon as their plane reached the gate and the seatbelt sign went off, Grady sprang to his feet. After an eternity cramped with his knees to his chest in a plane seat Houdini would have found trouble squeezing into, Grady was anxious to stretch. His eyelids felt like burlap coated their insides and his teeth felt much the same. It would be hours before he could close off the world with a hotel door and sleep. He and his parents had to fight their way out of the airport first. Still, it was great to be in Europe or it would be if he ever got off the airplane. He opened the overhead bin and helped Earl remove the family's violet travel bags, narrowly missing the head of a man in a baseball cap.

The doors opened and the crowd began to plod toward the exit. Eventually Grady made it out of the plane and onto the jet way. The stallions of enthusiasm urged him forward but he reined them back to match his parents' slow pace. Grady, Rowan, and Earl exited the ramp and followed signs directing new arrivals down stairs and through a corridor into a cavernous room where immigration officers waited at their booths. Earl paused with a bleary, confused stare until Grady pointed to the line for non-EU passport holders. All signs were in Gaelic first and then in English. No photography! No cell phones! Clutching passports and the entry cards they'd filled out on the plane, they followed the line that snaked between crowd-control posts and ropes bringing them face to face over and over again with a bearded man in a green sweatshirt that said Philadelphia Eagles and Irish.

The queue moved but not as quickly as Grady would have liked. After a dozen or so hours on a cramped airplane he wanted a bathroom all to himself, a shower, and clean sheets. Soon they were at the front standing behind a yellow line painted on the floor and waiting for the next available agent. Grady looked back and forth. None of the arriving passengers dared step on the barrier for fear of angering the official. Would the bureaucrat throw them out if he stepped over without permission? Grady inched his toe onto the line.

A man in a uniform motioned to them. Earl handed over their

passports. The man examined the pictures and typed at his keyboard. The huge, silver stamp made three loud thunks as he place the entry date on each passport and freed them to step through the sliding doors and into Europe.

"I'm going to change some money." Grady went to the Bank of Ireland counter and exchanged two hundred dollars for euros.

Meanwhile Rowan asked for directions to their hotel at the information booth and returned with pocket maps of Dublin. Following instructions, the Evans rolled their suitcases out of the terminal and followed the signs. When crossing the road to the shuttle-bus island Grady realized all his instincts were wrong in this country where people drove on the left side. He forced himself to look right for oncoming traffic but feared a car coming from the opposite direction would mow him down from behind. Finally he swiveled his head back and forth, not sure what direction vehicles would come from, and somehow crossed to safety.

It was overcast and chilly. While Earl bought tickets at a kiosk, Grady removed a hoody from his suitcase and put it on. Within seconds he was too hot and rolled the top of his hoody off his shoulders to let the sweat evaporate.

The bus came. They loaded their bags into the cargo bay and climbed aboard. Rowan and Earl sat in front. Grady had to walk to the back before he found an empty seat next to an old woman in a tan raincoat. The seats had seatbelts and shoulder straps but none of the passengers wore them. The bus pulled away. Soon it left the airport greenery and entered the city. At each stop the driver got out to open the cargo bay for departing passengers.

So this was Europe. Grady looked out the window at storefronts. The people dressed casually in nylon jackets and sweatshirts, no business suits or fancy dresses. The bus passed a store with cakes in the window called the Irish Yeast Company. It had to be a bakery. A store couldn't stay in business just selling yeast. Could it?

"Trinity College!" The driver stopped behind another bus next to the gray, stone walls.

"How do we get to Pearse?" Rowan asked after they retrieved their luggage.

"Go around college," the driver said in a Polish accent. "Just keep wall on your right."

Grady's suitcase wheels clicked rhythmically against the sidewalk as he rolled it after his parents. They passed the Yeast Company and a construction area with torn up asphalt behind orange, plastic netting. There was a sign for aikido in a second-story window. Rowan followed addresses until they arrived at their hotel, which was located above a pub with a red-lacquer front, gold lettering, and potted flowers hanging above the plate glass window.

Their rooms were not ready. After leaving their bags in the drawing room Rowan and Earl decided to eat brunch in the pub downstairs but the lure of exploration was too much for Grady to resist. He retraced his steps back to Trinity College and followed the signs for the Book of Kells, an eighth-century illuminated manuscript of the gospels. Inside the courtyard a line of tourists stretched from the entrance and along three walls. It was too much to deal with on so little sleep so Grady wandered through the campus of green lawns and gray, stone buildings. A student guide in a brown, sleeveless jacket with strips of cloth dangling over his arms addressed a group of tourists in front of a stone gazebo with an onion-shaped roof. Grady found a bathroom in the basement of the student union. Feeling better he left campus to wander along Grafton Street.

He was hot again so he slung his hoody over his shoulder as he entered the pedestrian mall lined with buskers and mimes in black makeup and black clothing. Grady ditched his American coins in the latter's basket as it would be months before he could spend them. Grady amused himself by checking out restaurant menus and eventually settled on a pub offering a full Irish breakfast. A woman stood behind taps for Guinness, Budweiser, Carlsberg, and Heineken. There were no signs asking customers to wait to be seated and Grady didn't know the protocol.

"Irish breakfast?" he asked.

"Just sit anywhere," the bartender said. "Anything to drink?"

Grady responded with the phrase all Americans have learned to associate with Ireland. "Pint of Guinness."

Evidently the drinking age was lower than in the states because the bartender didn't bat an eye or ask to see an ID. She filled a glass from the tap and set it down when it was three quarters full.

"Just letting it settle," she said.

Grady took a seat at a table that wasn't too close or too far away. The bartender brought his Guinness and set the glass on a coaster in front of him. Grady looked down. She'd formed the figure of a clover in the foam. It was so skillful that Grady was reluctant to drink it but he did. The carbonation was less harsh than in America. Grady set the glass down to save it for his meal and wiped foam from his lips. At the nearby table, two old guys were talking about their hospital stays. Grady looked through the finger-sized, foil packets of sauces – ketchup, mustard, mayonnaise, malt vinegar, and brown sauce.

"Here you are." The bartender set a massive plate in front of him.

There were eggs, ham, sausage, potatoes, beans, a fried tomato, and something that resembled a sausage patty but was actually a black pudding. Grady tried the brown sauce on his potatoes. It tasted like steak sauce so he poured some on his eggs too. Once he finished the hearty meal, he paid and left only small coins for a tip, tipping being not really done in Europe.

He looked in a few shop windows and browsed a crowded bookstore before returning to the hotel. He had a small room with a bed, TV, chair, and mercifully an attached bathroom. Grady stripped off his clothes and washed up in the cramped shower. The thick quilt on the bed was too hot for summer so he lay uncovered and used the remote to tune the TV to RTE 1. Planning to nap a few hours Grady closed his eyes. He'd just nap for a few hours. Just a few hours…

Grady woke in the dark and checked his watch. It was 11:00 PM and he was hungry. There was no point in waking his parents so he pulled on his jeans. He sniffed the long-sleeved shirt he'd worn on the plane, tossed it in the plastic bag, and put on his dark blue polo shirt. His passport and American dollars went in the money belt, which he put on before zipping his pants. His shirtfront bulged. He positioned the money belt lower on his hips so the waist of his pants would keep it from showing. Awkward as hell but he'd better get used to it. He'd be wearing it for the next twelve months. Outside he headed toward the circle and triangle logo of a Spar convenience store, a few blocks away, and entered to explore the unfamiliar candy and cookies on its shelves. With so much to look at he must have seemed strange. There were pastries, beer, Insomnia coffee, sodas, and an ice cream bar called Magnum. Grady bought a chocolate croissant, chicken piri-piri sandwich, and a few tangerines. Rather than fumbling with coins he paid the South-Asian clerk with a ten-euro note and let him make change.

When he returned to his room, he found that piri-piri was a kind of hot sauce. After finishing the sandwich he peeled and ate a tangerine, brushed his teeth, and cycled through TV shows with the remote. Grady settled on a movie where Andie MacDowell trades houses with a woman from Dublin but he fell asleep before the end.

Grady woke to a knock on his door. It was Rowan.

"Get ready. We need to hurry to see the Book of Kells."

Grady dressed and met his parents downstairs.

"You sleep?" Earl asked.

"Fourteen hours," Grady said.

They returned to Trinity College. This time there were only a dozen people waiting, all with the same guidebook Rowan had. The Evans got in line behind three teenagers who spoke French and waited for the exhibit to open.

"If we spend an hour here that will give us an hour at the National Museum of Archeology before lunch." Rowan turned a page in her guide book. "In the afternoon we can walk up O'Connell Street and see the James Joyce Center."

"What about the Guinness Brewery?" Earl winked at Grady.

"It doesn't have as many stars," Rowan said.

After twenty minutes the line started moving. Earl paid the entry fees and Grady followed his parents into the exhibit. The room contained blowups from the manuscript with explanatory text. Grady read a few of the descriptions before quitting in frustration with the other tourists who got in his way. Before giving up, he learned about an old script consisting of parallel lines and that scribes had written the manuscripts on animal skins with inks that came from oak galls (whatever they were). He wanted nothing more than to see the book and get out but his parents were intent on reading all the background material no matter how long it took.

Grady skipped ahead, walked into the darkened room with the case that contained two volumes of the Book of Kells, and leaned his elbows on the glass to look. On top of one page was a figure of an apostle along with lines of hand-written script that he couldn't make out. He assumed it was in Latin but even reading the letters was difficult. Grady moved to the other volume and had roughly three minutes before tourists crowded him out.

A book from 800 AD was pretty remarkable he supposed but he wasn't Catholic and it didn't have much resonance with him. Grady returned to the exhibit and stood waiting for his parents. They needed to work out a system where he could move at his own pace or this waiting would drive him crazy.

"Did you see the book?" Grady motioned to the darkened room once his parents were ready.

He followed them inside and waited while they looked. They all exited into a library with a long, vaulted ceiling but by then it was too crowded to see anything. They went to the next attraction. Grady had to wait for his parents at the Book of Kells exhibit but in the National Museum-Archeology it was their turn. He lost track of time once he saw bronze cauldrons and spear points from 2000 BC. The shapes were symmetric as anything turned out by a factory but he didn't know anything about the people who'd created them. Why had no one taught him about the Celts in high school? Grady moved on to display cases full of crescent-shaped necklaces of flattened gold and bracelets that resembled horns bent into U's.

"Grady." Rowan approached from behind and rested a hand on his shoulder.

"Time to go already?"

"Earl and I are going to lunch but you can stay as long as you like." She took a twenty-euro note from her purse and gave it to him. "Buy yourself some lunch and meet us back at the hotel around dinner time. Can you find your way back?"

Grady nodded absentmindedly and turned back to the display. There were Viking and medieval artifacts but he was more interested in prehistory so he circled back to a tomb made of piled rocks before examining copper axes and bones carved with geometric patterns. What did those people believe?

Whatever it was, it was not benign. In the next room he found a dozen excited boy scouts and their adult leader all in shorts, khaki shirts, and hats along with an exhibit about human sacrifice. The lights were dim and three separate walled areas held bog mummies in display cases. These were nobles who had been killed and thrown into peat bogs. The bogs preserved the bodies leaving them shriveled and the color of beef jerky.

After several hours at the museum Grady wandered around the trendy neighborhood called Temple Bar looking for someplace to eat. Most of the meals on menus posted outside pubs and restaurants ran about fourteen euros. There was a place selling meat pies but Grady wanted to sit down. He settled on an Iranian restaurant that served him a huge, open-faced pita with barbecued chicken, lettuce, tomato, pickled beets, and hot sauce for roughly eight euros. Exiting the Temple Bar, he crossed the River Liffey and strolled O'Connell Street passing the post office that featured in the 1916 Easter Uprising and a tall spire that seemed to pierce the clouds. After stopping at a Costa Coffee he returned to the hotel and watched the BBC and Sky TV for a few hours before knocking on his parents' door.

"Hi Grady," Earl peeked into the hallway from the gap in the barely open door. "Your mother needs a little time to get ready. We'll stop by your room in a half hour or so."

Hair wet from the shower and skins flushed they showed up at Grady's door forty-five minutes later. Rowan wore a skirt and shawl while Earl dressed in khaki slacks and a pale blue shirt.

"Let's find a place with live music," Rowan said.

The three went to Temple Bar and selected a pub for dinner. Earl ordered Irish stew, Grady chicken curry, and Rowan smoked salmon.

"Something to drink?" the waitress asked.

"Pint of Guinness," Earl said.

"Make that two," Rowan added.

"Guess I'll just have a glass of water," Grady said.

"Nonsense!" Earl said. "If you're man enough to travel the world, you're man enough to have a beer! Pint of Guinness for my son!"

While they ate a musician wearing jeans and an unbuttoned, plaid shirt over a black T-shirt set up his guitar and microphone. Gray streaked his beard and shoulder-length hair. Grady guessed he was in his late forties. Once he perched on the stool and adjusted the mike, he spoke to the audience.

"How you doin', tonight?" The musician had a mid-western, American accent, maybe Chicago. "I'm Art Rabsey and here's a song many of you will remember."

The opening guitar notes intrigued Grady but he lost interest fast when he realized it was "Hotel California." Art had a strong voice but to earn Grady's respect, a real musician had to write his own songs. From their response the audience didn't agree. Neither did Grady's parents. Earl draped an arm over Rowan's shoulder and they both got misty eyed swaying to the rhythm. Art finished and launched into another Eagles hit "Take It Easy." A man from the audience placed a pint of Guinness at Art's feet.

"You know, Guinness is like milk," Art said between songs.

"Without all that carbonation it goes down easy and you can get really drunk."

Grady hoped for an original song but it was not to be. Art sang "Horse with No Name," "Sister Golden Hair," "Dancing in the Moonlight," and "The Boys Are Back in Town." It wasn't horrible but it wasn't brilliant. He was a competent guitarist and Grady liked his version of "Wonderwall" but it wasn't the vibrant, Irish music Grady had come to expect. He ordered another Guinness. His parents didn't seem to mind and dulling his senses was the only way to get through the night. Art was also collecting Guinness. By now audience members had set three pints at his feet.

"No more!" Art bellowed when a man in a knit cap approached with another pint. "I mean it." The man set the pint at Art's feet anyway. "Does anybody want a free pint?" Art held up the glass and gave it to a blonde woman.

The night seemed to go on forever. Grady tolerated several hours but when Art launched into "Bye Bye Miss American Pie," Grady could take no more. Much as he was dying to make a sarcastic remark, he didn't want to spoil his mother's bliss.

"Hey dad." Grady leaned his mouth to Earl's ear. "I'm a little jet lagged. I'm going back to the hotel." Grady stood.

"Grady, are you okay?" Rowan asked. "Want us to go with you?"

"No, just a little tired. I had a great time. See you, tomorrow."

The next day they took a two-and-a-half-hour bus ride to Galway on the west coast.

"It's where my great grandfather came from," Rowan said.

"Are you going to look up our relatives?" Grady asked.

"We'll see."

The countryside of trees and grass looked pretty ordinary to Grady but closer to Galway he saw stone fences and a man exercising a horse on a lead. Once they got into town, they checked into a hotel near Eyre Square. Galway was a pleasant city with winding, cobblestone streets and plenty of shops and restaurants. The fish and chips place was good and the local, seafood chowder was excellent. The weather could not make up its mind forcing Grady to carry a hoody, umbrella, and sunglasses to cover all eventualities. Rowan made no effort to look up relatives. Instead she walked along the river admiring bridges, stone buildings, and the parallel canal. After a few days Grady began to wonder what they were doing there.

"Your mother needs a little time to herself," Earl said. "Let's go see the Aran Islands, just the two of us."

Grady and Earl took the morning ferry to Inishmore and rented mountain bikes from a shop near the docks. The roads were narrow and they had to yield when a horse-drawn buggy or tour bus approached. At first finding directions was difficult but there weren't many roads and soon they were on their way to the two-thousand-year-old fort, Dún Aenghus. They rode through countryside that was mostly green fields broken up by fences made of loose, gray stones. Grady saw no trees.

Despite his age Earl kept up with Grady but was winded by the time they parked their bikes at the Dún Aenghus visitors' center. It was early but already a mob of Japanese tourists disembarked from two tour buses. Grady and Earl paid the entry fee, skipped the displays, and rushed onto the trail to the fort. Surrounded by grass, bushes, and flowers; under cloudy skies; and out of sight of other tourists Grady began to feel the landscape's magic. Beautiful but how could anybody earn a living on this desolate island? He wanted to linger but the voices of the approaching tourists spurred him on.

As they climbed Grady began to sweat so he took off his hoody. They passed a clearing and approached the outer wall of loose, gray stones that was about as tall as two men.

"How did they build this thing?" Grady rested a hand on the cool stone. "How did they get food and water up here? What did they eat?"

"And these stones." Earl touched one. "Do you suppose they had to cut them into blocks or did they come out of the ground like this?"

They kept going until they entered a low passage through the innermost wall that surrounded them on three sides. The fourth was a cliff overlooking the Atlantic. Grady approached but grew fearful close to the edge. The ground was limestone with a few puddles and patches of green moss. He squatted and then lay flat on his belly to look over the side. It dropped straight down to the gray, ocean water. Climbing the cliff or running up the hill with a sword – either way it would be hell trying to attack this place.

The Japanese tourists arrived. Contrary to Gray's fears they did not prove annoying. Mostly they took pictures and helped each other get views over the edge.

"*Kore wa Ireland no Himeji desu*," Grady said to an old man in a yellow, baseball cap who smiled at Grady's joke.

Grady and Earl sat content with the fresh air and sound of the breeze while admiring the view. They could see all the way across the island but haze shrouded the houses and stone walls in the distance. After an hour Earl said, "Ready to go?" They hiked down to the visitors' center, had sandwiches, biked a bit more, and returned on the 5:00 ferry.

"It's time to go," Rowan said when they got back to Galway.

The next day they took the bus to Dublin and caught a flight to London.

At Heathrow a half dozen skinny men held cardboard signs with the names of lucky arrivals, whose ground transportation was assured, printed in magic marker. Beyond them the airport was a mass of moving humanity. The racial mix astounded Grady. Middle-Eastern families the women in headscarves, South Asians, and Caribbean blacks were as numerous as Caucasians.

Earl stopped at a currency exchange, came back with several pound notes, and gave a few to Grady and Rowan.

"The guidebook says we're supposed to catch a bus to Bath." Earl stuffed the remaining notes in his wallet. "Can you tell where it is?"

Grady looked around but the signs were confusing. Earl approached a man in a Sikh turban and aquamarine information blazer.

"Excuse me. Where do we catch the bus for Bath?"

"Follow the signs down the ramp and out door number three," the Sikh said with an accent that could have come from a BBC announcer.

The bus stop consisted of several lanes separated by concrete islands. Grady examined the signs and found the waiting area for Bath while Earl went to buy tickets. Rowan sat like a bag of onions on a bench under a rain cover and rummaged in her purse for a pack of cigarettes.

"Excuse me." She waved her cigarette at a man with a spiky rubber backpack. "Do you have a light?"

The man produced a propane lighter. Rowan took a deep drag that turned the tip into a half-inch of glowing ash as she leaned back as if falling into a feather bed after a tiring day. Grady moved out of the path of the smoke. Moments later Rowan bent forward with a cough that rattled her chest. Earl returned with the tickets and averted his eyes from the irritating sight of his wife's continued smoking.

The bus to Bath arrived with a hiss of airbrakes and rumble of its diesel engine. Rowan stubbed out her cigarette and the three boarded. The ride took two hours. Grady found the countryside uninteresting, flat and grassy with a few rolling hills. They passed through towns with dirty brick row houses that were as dreary as the BBC situation comedies the public TV station showed back home. Grady cataloged the different makes of cars and was amazed at the number of Peugeots.

They arrived in Bath and drove along the River Avon that was spanned by stone bridges. Earl flagged down a taxi, which took them to a pleasant building with a wrought-iron railing by the steps leading to the front door. They registered and Grady hauled his bag up the narrow stairway to his room on the second floor. After a shower in the bathroom down the hall, he changed clothes, grabbed his hoody, descended the stairs, and followed the sound of voices to the lobby.

"What part of California are you from, then?" a woman's voice asked.

"It's in the south," Rowan said, "by the border with Mexico."

"Must be frightfully hot."

Grady reached the bottom of the stairs and turned the corner. His mother was standing near the opening to the kitchen.

"Oh Grady, this is Mrs. Fuller." Rowan gestured to the middle-aged woman behind the counter. "She and her husband own the inn."

"Nice to meet ya, Grady." Mrs. Fuller dried her hand on her apron and extended it for Grady to shake.

"We were talking about things to do in Bath." Rowan pointed to sites on the map spread on the counter. "Kate says we should see the costume museum after taking in the Roman ruins."

"We also have country music at the Chisholm Trail Club on Monmouth." Mrs. Fuller pointed to a flier on the wall-mounted rack.

"Bizarre," Grady said.

"Maybe we can go check it out after dinner." Rowan put the flier in her purse.

"What about dad?"

"Asleep. Can you believe it? I'm the sick one and he's acting like an invalid. Come on, Grady. Let's see what kind of nightlife this town offers."

Grady and Rowan left the inn and set out in search of a restaurant. The sidewalks were not crowded in the residential area. Houses were neat, multistory affairs with a small lawn in front and little space between them. Cars were parallel-parked along the road.

They came to a crosswalk and Rowan pushed the button.

"Isn't it wonderful, Grady?" She spread her arms as if she were going to fly and wrapped them around him. "Everything's so different and new. I feel reborn."

"I feel like I'll go into a coma if I don't get something to eat."

The crossing speaker chirped. Rowan released him from her bear hug and they continued their journey, passing several Italian and sushi restaurants deemed too expensive. They encountered a wooden sign for a pub called the Red Lion that pictured the animal.

"Let's see how the English pubs differ from the Irish." Rowan pushed through the door. Grady followed.

Inside a half-dozen patrons sat at the bar with their pints of chocolate-brown Guinness. A few children among the customers sat at the tables and even a German shepherd wandering around their feet. Rowan found a free table. The menu, chalked on the blackboard behind the bar, included fish and chips, sandwiches, and something called mushy peas. They waited. After fifteen minutes no waitress had come to the table.

"Maybe we need to order at the bar," Rowan said.

They got up and stood by the cash register. The bartender, a lanky man with a graying mustache, turned from the soccer match on the black-and-white TV.

"Help you?"

"We'll have two orders of fish and chips with the mushy peas," Rowan said. "And can you recommend a good local beer?"

"Stout, bitter, or lager?"

"Oh, I don't know. A stout. I guess."

"Well, there's Theakston Old Peculiar on draught. That's my favorite."

"Okay, we'll have two of those."

"Pints or halves?"

"The half pints."

"That'll be ten pounds fifty." The bartender pulled two glasses and scribbled the food order for the kitchen.

Rowan paid and they returned to their table. The beer wasn't so much warm as cool. Behind the bitterness was an intriguing herbal taste that would have been obliterated, had it been served at polar temperatures. After finishing his, Grady wanted another.

The food came. The fish and chips were pretty much what Grady had expected but the mushy peas were a disgusting dollop of green glop that he couldn't bring himself to sample. He picked the breading off the fish, went light on the chips, returned to the bar, and ordered another pint along with a half for Rowan. When he returned he reached across the table to turn Rowan's butter knife so its tip didn't point at his heart.

"Why do you always do that?" she asked.

"In samurai culture you never point a blade at anyone," Grady said repeating Sensei Wakayama's words. "Even in flower arranging they twist the leaves so the edge faces away from the viewer."

"Sounds kind of OCD, like you're afraid some kind of invisible death ray will shoot out and give you cancer." She turned the butter knife back to its original position.

"That's ridiculous." Grady folded his used napkin into a neat rectangle and set it beside his plate.

After dinner they located the country and western dance bar and paid the cover charge to enter. Rowan found a free place to stand. From their spot near the wall they watched the local band, The Buckingham Buckaroos, four pasty-faced guys in black cowboy hats playing slide guitar, bass, and drums. Rowan leaned close and yelled in Grady's ear.

"Maybe we could ask someone to teach us how to do the dances."

Grady would rather shrink to the size of a cockroach and crawl between the stomping cowboy boots to some hideaway. It was bad enough escorting his mom and being the only one not dressed like a hick. Did they have to ask strangers for lessons too?

A short man wearing a belt buckle the size of a Dodge RAM 3500 bumper sauntered over.

"Say partner, would it cheese you off if I ask your sister to dance?"

Grady dismissed his mother with a wave of his hand. The Cotswold cowboy escorted her to the dance floor's outer ring where two-steppers orbited the central mass of line dancers. While his mother danced with a succession of cowboys, Grady stared at women. Most wore jeans faded in strategic spots. He went to the bar and caught the bartender's eye.

"Let me have an Old Peculiar."

"Sorry, sir. We don't have that brand."

"How about a Guinness?" Grady asked.

"Do you have some identification?"

Grady produced his wallet but for some reason the bartender wouldn't give him a beer. Grady went back to his spot by the wall with a cola and a bad attitude. Rowan returned flushed, winded, and smiling. She tugged at Grady's shoulder.

"Ask someone to dance."

"I'm tired," he said. "Can we go?"

The walk back was more effort that Rowan wanted to try so they took a cab.

"You seem awfully grumpy," she said after she'd given the driver their destination. "What's your problem?"

Grady looked at the back of the driver's head and said, "Nothing."

"Nothing? Jesus Grady, you've been brooding ever since we decided to go on this trip. I wish you'd just tell me what's wrong, instead of making everybody else miserable."

"Miserable?" Grady snorted. "I didn't even want to come."

Rowan sniffed, wiped her eyes with the back of her hand, and turned away to stare out the window. Grady went over possible options from *Aikido in Everyday Life* but none of the triangles, circles, or squares told him how to deal with a crying woman. He glanced at the rearview mirror and saw the driver's eyes dart away.

"Mom." Grady rested a hand on Rowan's shoulder. "I'm sorry."

"Just shut up, Grady." She brushed his hand away.

CHAPTER 5

OBgrrl@yahoo.com
Dear Grady,
How was your flight? I bet you're glad to get out of that sardine can after 12 hours, huh? I guess you must be in Ireland now.

My mom was waiting up for me when I got back. We kind of got into it but things worked out okay. She always liked you, Grady, and she kind of let it slide because you were going away. Speaking of moms, how's yours?

Only a week & I already miss you. Can't wait to visit in August. Today, I'm going to the mall and apply for a job. Gotta earn some money for the trip.

Let me know about Ireland. I'm dying to hear about the music, the people, and all those pints of Guinness.

Bye Puffins,
Marisol

gsankyu@hotmail.com
Dear Marisol,
We're not in Ireland. We're about 100 km SW of London in Bath. Mom's doing really great! All we had to do was get her away from those doctors & hospitals, and she turned into a ball of energy.

Today we saw baths the Romans built on top of hot springs in 43 AD. There's an old temple and a courtyard that encloses the baths. Even though the water's supposed to be healing, there are all these signs telling you not to touch it. Didn't stop mom, though. She stuck her hands in the bath, ladled water over her shoulders, and even splashed some on her face. A guard had to ask her to stop. I could have died.

All these Roman ruins are just a preview of what we'll see in August. I'm really psyched.

Love,
Grady
PS I hear the ice cream's really great in Italy, too.

Grady lifted his hands off the keyboard and looked at the other patrons in the Internet café. A girl in thick, black glasses sat hunched over the computer nearest him. Farther away three pimply teenaged boys appeared to be playing some kind of role-playing game. Grady logged out of his e-mail account and paid the attendant. It was nearly 6:30. His parents had talked about eating dinner at a Thai place around 8:00 but Grady was going to grab a snack and tell them he wasn't hungry. That way he could escape a few hours of his mother's stony silence. He stopped at a café that was a cut above fast food and had a bit more local color too with a set of glass-covered tables each with a flower in the dining area. Grady examined the menu board, ordered a baked potato stuffed with shrimp at the counter, and sat down.

"Excuse me, sir," the woman said. "Were you going to eat that here?"

"Yeah."

"I'll have to charge you a pound extra. Five fifty is the takeaway price."

Grady stared at her. Was she joking? Apparently not. He got up, handed over the extra money, and sat back down. She brought his meal. The cook had dumped an entire bottle of greasy, pink salad dressing over his baked potato and shrimp. Grady scraped off as much of the glop as he could and choked down the rest but it would be easier to digest a leather coat. He wouldn't want to eat again for over twelve hours.

The light at the crosswalk outside the café seemed a perfect place to put Grady's first international OBEY Giant sticker. He peeled off the backing and attached it to the metal box that housed the button.

"Hey!" an old man in a flat cap yelled at him. "What do you think you're doing? Get that off of there right now!"

The light changed and Grady dashed across the street. He crossed Pulteney Bridge and strolled along the banks of the River Avon where teams of big-shouldered women practiced rowing in colorful shells. The setting sun's light warmed the facades of the limestone buildings. As the warm breeze ruffled his hair with gentle fingers, Grady let go of his annoyance with Rowan. A group of Africans in purple dashikis sang and danced for tips on Broad Street. Grady took a left on George and cut through the park. A Labrador retriever approached and dropped a soggy tennis ball at his feet. Grady threw it and the dog gave chase.

"Thanks," said the dog's owner a pale, freckled, red-haired man.

Grady passed the crescent-shaped townhouses and wondered if Jane Austen had lived in one. After a quick jaunt up Church Street he was back at the hotel. He begged off dinner with his parents and retreated to his room to wash his shirts in the sink and watch TV. Instead of showing wacky British comedies all the BBC offered that night were recycled American cop shows.

Grady was about ready to go to sleep when his parents knocked on his door. He'd forgotten it was Sunday night, time for their weekly poker game. It didn't matter that they were overseas; the ritual had to go on. Rowan dealt cards onto his bedspread. She hadn't brought enough pennies so they augmented their stakes with British pence. Grady played his usual conservative game and managed not to lose to his mother as badly as Earl did. At 11:30 Earl swept all the coins off Grady's bedspread and left with Rowan.

Rowan and Earl held hands on the bus trip to Stonehenge. Grady didn't want to speculate on the cause of their big, dopey grins but it was good to see them happy. Rowan rested her head on Earl's shoulder and closed her eyes.

Now that he was more awake than on the trip from the airport, Grady was able to concentrate on the road signs. He learned that a divided highway was called a dual carriageway. He also saw a puzzling sign for traffic calming, which turned out to be a traffic circle used to slow cars down.

They needed to change buses at Salisbury where a cathedral's gray spire was visible from the station. Mrs. Fuller had said it was worth a look so they walked over. Rowan limped. The knee she'd twisted dancing was still bothering her. Once inside the grounds Earl stopped and aimed his digital camera at the graceful, stone structure.

"Pretty remarkable when you realize they built it all with chisels, pulleys, and levers almost eight hundred years ago," he said.

"It almost looks like it can fly." Rowan lit a cigarette and took a few quick puffs.

The camera's zoom lens extended and retracted under battery power until Earl was satisfied with the picture's composition. He clicked the shutter.

As they approached, Grady got a feel for the cathedral's scale. The spire was over four hundred feet tall. He'd learned about cathedrals in history but the dry discussion in his textbooks hadn't prepared him for this. He couldn't imagine the dedication it would have taken to build such a structure.

Once inside they passed the church lady at the donation desk and gazed at the vaulted ceiling that arched like a medieval view of heaven over them. In the cathedral's center, stone pillars buckled under the weight of the spire. Grady put on his hoody as the stone walls kept the interior cool. A medieval clock, a clunky device of pulleys and gears, squatted in the corner.

"Tower's over a hundred meters high" Earl said. "Figuring the density of rock it must weigh at least five thousand tons. Wonder how they kept it standing so long."

Rowan sat to rest her sore joints and Grady took a seat beside her. Although sermons and choral music left him cold, here the very air seemed to vibrate with a quiet sense of awe. Grady imagined all the cathedrals in Europe, the effort it had taken to build them, and all the people who had worshipped inside. Then he pictured German Stuka dive-bombers during the Battle of Britain and realized how easy these masterpieces were to destroy. He imagined himself in an RAF uniform or as a knight in chain mail riding out with a cruciform sword to defend against the Mongol invasion.

Rowan tapped him on the shoulder. They continued their clockwise walk passing the high altar and tombs of bishops and noblemen, exited out onto the cloister, and followed the signs into the Chapter House where an original Magna Carta was on display.

"Wow," Grady stared at the parchment behind thick glass.

"Says here there are only four original copies left." Earl pointed to the pamphlet he'd picked up at the entrance.

"You read about stuff like this in history books and suddenly here it is." Rowan played absent-mindedly with the zipper on her jacket.

"We just don't have things this old in America." Earl tried to take a picture but it was too dim.

"What about the Anastasi ruins?" Rowan asked.

"They're not the same," Earl said.

Grady agreed but wasn't sure why. They stared at the Magna Carta and tried to puzzle out Western democracy's beginning from its Latin script. Then sensing the futility of their efforts they decided to go but were unable to walk away without feeling they weren't giving this treasure its due.

Stonehenge was smaller than Grady had expected. Even though it was visible from the highway, Earl paid the entry fee at the visitors' center and the three walked under the overpass to the grass-covered field where the ancient stone columns stood. In a strange contrast, modern druid wannabes pointed Y-shaped dowsing rods at the earth while fighter jets from a nearby RAF base streaked overhead. A rope fence kept tourists from approaching the stones. Grady and his parents made one circle of the structure and then another before catching the return bus. A sign at the exit reminded visitors to drive on the left.

They returned to Bath in the late afternoon and took the train to London the next morning. After his experience with at the crossing light Grady lost his desire to post OBEY Giant stickers. He couldn't find Japanese green tea anywhere, only black. They might have had some in the Starbucks that seemed to have sprouted on every corner but Grady couldn't bring himself to enter. He wasn't sure what London had more of - American tourists or closed-circuit TV security cameras that watched everyone through unblinking lenses. The Brits they'd talked to didn't seem to mind Big Brother's constant attention. In fact, they seemed to welcome it. Grady and his parents were staying in a small bed and breakfast in Notting Hill.

"I go to Paris and like it well enough," the owner had said to Earl, "but there's nothing like London, sir. There's nothing like London."

Grady and his parents rushed around the city. They saw a play in Leicester Square, stood under the giant dome of St. Paul's Cathedral, and roamed the seemingly endless halls of artifacts at the British Museum. These included giant stone griffins from Babylon and statues looted from the Parthenon. At the Tower of London a tour guide, dressed in a black-and-red Beefeater uniform, mentioned that prisoners had to pay for their room and board.

"I wonder how long it'll take before our politicians adopt that practice," Rowan muttered.

"Shh." Earl put a finger to his lips. "Don't give them any ideas."

Grady learned that the Globe Theater used cow hair in its plaster and that patrons urinated in the audience during Shakespeare's day. They rode the London Eye Ferris wheel. He saw one of Salvador Dali's lobster telephones at the Tate Modern. The artist had half expected the waiter to bring a melted telephone whenever he ordered lobster in a restaurant.

Rowan had a crush on the Naked Chef, Jamie Oliver. She'd read that he worked at a restaurant in the suburbs, called the River Café so she persuaded Grady and Earl to travel off the page of the London map. The trip to the London Underground's Hammersmith Station was not difficult. They took the District Line to Earl's Court and transferred to the Piccadilly Line, which emerged from the tunnel into the daylight of suburbia with its train tracks and overhead wires. They got off at the station and the silver train pulled away. Earl looked around at the confusion of shopping centers and office buildings.

"Now what?" he asked.

"I bet it's this way." Following his intuition Grady led the others down a major thoroughfare.

The walked for fifteen minutes and stopped in front of Charing Cross Hospital. Rowan looked at the industrial park across the street.

"This doesn't seem right," she said. "It must be on the other side of the bridge, we saw outside the station."

They retraced their steps and crossed the bridge over the Thames. By now Grady's stomach was rumbling like a coffee percolator. The only restaurants he saw on this side of the river were fish and chips shops and a Japanese place. Rowan approached a policeman. He was tall and blonde with striking blue eyes.

"Excuse me, could you tell us where the River Café is?"

"Of course." He pointed back across the bridge. "Go to the flyover and take a right. You can't miss it."

"Thanks." Rowan and the others walked away. "What's a flyover?" she asked.

"Beats me," Grady said. "Let's get sushi."

"We could take a cab." Rowan, who had started to limp, pointed to a taxi stand.

"Look," Earl said. "The River Café has to be on the river. Right? We know which side it's on. I say we walk along the bank until we find it."

They crossed the bridge and were in front of the hospital a second time.

"Rowan!" A woman in a loose, checked pullover waved from across the street.

"Oh my god! Sheila!" Rowan jumped up and down and dashed to the crosswalk.

Earl moved at a slower pace. By the time the light changed, he was still too far away to cross. While he and Grady waited for the light to cycle, Rowan embraced her friend on the other side of the street and was pointing back at them. Grady and his father crossed and approached the women. Sheila had a pudgy face, had short streaked hair that was dark at the roots, and wore a choker of large purple beads.

"Sheila, this is my son, Grady, and you remember Earl."

"Hello, Sheila." Earl's tone dripped distaste.

"Still keeping the war machine well oiled, Earl?"

"Sheila was the lead singer for Dollhouse Underground, Grady." Rowan took hold of Sheila's hands. "They played some of the same clubs as we did in DC."

"Until my visa expired and I had to return to the UK," Sheila said. "Speaking of which, why are you here?"

"We're taking a year off to travel around the world," Grady said.

"But shouldn't you be in school?"

"He graduated from high school this month, and learning about other cultures before college will be an invaluable experience. Nice seeing you again, Sheila." Earl turned away.

"Do you know where the River Café is?" Rowan asked.

"It's right around the corner," Sheila said.

"If you aren't doing anything else," Rowan said, "maybe you'd like to join us for lunch."

"Let me check my busy social calendar." Sheila looked at her watch. "Nope, nothing planned. I'd love to."

Sheila led them into the industrial park where they found the River Café perched on the banks of the Thames. The hostess sat them in a courtyard overlooking the blue waters.

"Good Lord!" Earl examined the menu. "These entrees are fifty bucks!"

Sheila smirked.

"After coming all this way, I'm not going back until I've had a decent meal." Rowan folded her menu and set in on the table.

The waitress brought bread. Grady chose something called John Dory, Rowan ordered salmon, and Earl lamb. When Sheila chose the steak Florentine, Earl scowled. It was the most expensive dish on the menu.

"Is Jamie Oliver working, today?" Rowan asked.

"Oh no, he left years back." The waitress scribbled the order on her notepad.

"Should we have wine?" Rowan asked.

"Why not?" Sheila spread her napkin on her lap.

The waitress brought the white wine Rowan selected, let Earl sample, and poured glasses all around. To Grady it tasted like vinegar but then he never was much of a connoisseur. Rowan and her friend caught up on old times while Earl sulked and Grady watched the boats on the sparkling waters of the Thames.

"So Sheila, whatever happened to you after you came back? Did you start another band?"

"I sang with Tony Scott and Mark Leed for a bit but we mostly played local pubs and gave up after a year. Vinyl Suicide did a cover of 'Razorblade Betty' in the nineties."

"I remember that song."

"Not much happened after that." Sheila sipped her wine. "I'm surprised you never broke through. Weren't you supposed to go on tour?"

"That fell apart."

"What happened?"

"Mitch." Rowan looked down at her bread.

Earl tensed at the mention of Rowan's former lead guitarist.

Sheila nodded. "Do you still keep in touch with him?"

"I heard he went into rehab after Earl and I got married."

"Do you play any instruments, Grady?" Sheila asked.

"I tried to teach him the bass," Rowan said, "but he's more interested in aikido."

"So if anyone gives us a hard time, you can beat them up?" Sheila said.

"It's not like that. It's..."

The waitress interrupted with their lunches. When Earl took a bite his scowl turned into a smile.

"Mmm." Earl waved a piece of lamb on the end of his fork as if conducting a symphony. "Not bad. Not bad at all."

Grady's fish was superb. Seared and topped with fresh rosemary, the filet was cooked to that magic moment when it was done but still tender. How could something so simple be so delicious? Rowan ordered another bottle of wine.

"This trip around the world sounds so marvelous." Sheila clapped her hands together. "Where are you going to go?"

"Europe, Australia, and then on to Japan," Rowan said.

"What? You're not going to India?"

"There's a State Department warning."

"Don't want to get in the middle of a nuclear war between India and Pakistan," Earl added.

"Oh, posh! Nikki and I spent two weeks in Goa and then went to a lovely little ashram in Kerala. Yoga practice started at 5:00 AM but they weren't pushy about it. You should definitely go." Sheila took her cell phone out of her purse. "I'll call Nikki and get the address."

"We can't take a chance on the sanitation," Earl said.

"A little case of traveler's diarrhea? You'll get over it." When no one replied, Sheila turned to Rowan. "You look kind of pale. Are you all right?"

"I've had some problems."

"What?"

"Cancer."

"Oh, Rowan. I'm so sorry." Sheila took hold of Rowan's hands. "They treated my friend Catherine at St. George's and she's doing very well. If you want I could find out who her doctor was."

"I'm fine, Sheila." Rowan removed her hands from her friend's grasp. "I finished my treatments and I feel great."

The discussion tapered off as they finished their meals. No one ordered desert. The bill came.

"Thank you for lunch." Sheila blotted her mouth with her napkin.

"Don't mention it." Earl paid with a credit card.

They walked toward the front door. Despite the awkwardness, the warm, summer air felt like a giant hand spreading peace in all directions.

"It was really good seeing you again." Sheila walked a few steps, paused, and turned back. "I don't suppose you'd like to come to dinner, tomorrow. Nikki and I share a small place in Belgravia."

"We'd love to," Rowan said.

Sheila and her partner lived north of Victoria Station on a street lined with tidy row houses. Grady, Rowan, and Earl arrived a little after 7:00, climbed the front steps, and rang the bell. A hefty blonde woman in a peasant skirt answered.

"You must be Sheila's friends. I'm Nikki. Welcome!" She smothered each of them in a big hug before showing them inside. A black cat with white paws paced into the entryway and circled their legs. "That's Simha." Nikki scratched the cat behind the ears and accepted the bottle of wine Rowan brought. "Why don't you sit in the living room while I check on Sheila? Hope you like curry."

From the living room it was obvious that Sheila had come a long way from her supposedly working-class, punk-rock background. The furniture was upscale and the walls were painted deep blue with geometric patterns near the ceiling and hardwood floor. The only remnant of her roots was the music collection that included the Buzzcocks, Joy Division, and Public Image Limited.

"I hope you didn't have too much trouble finding the place," Sheila said when she entered the room. "Dinner will be just a few minutes. What would you like to drink?"

Grady asked for a cup of tea and examined the bookshelf while his parents talked with Sheila. All the authors were women except for Michel Foucault. The doorbell rang.

"Oh hi, come on in." Sheila escorted a thin woman in a purple, knee-length dress into the living room. "I took the liberty of inviting my friend, Catherine Fletcher. Catherine, this is Rowan, Earl, and Grady."

"Good to meet you." Catherine extended her hand.

Rather than take it Rowan turned with a look of betrayal to Sheila.

"Dinner's ready!" Nikki called from the kitchen.

They carried their drinks to the dining room with Rowan walking more slowly than when she went for chemotherapy.

"This is chana masala." Nikki came in hauling a hot casserole with pot holders. "And with have muttar paneer, chutney, and raita."

They sat. Rowan toyed with her salad.

"Care of a pappadam?" Sheila passed a basket to Grady. The aromas were wonderful.

"Sheila tells me you're a cancer survivor," Catherine said.

"Lung." Rowan kept her eyes on her plate. "If you don't mind, this is a vacation and I'd rather leave the talk of illness at home."

"Having a support group of people who will listen has been essential to my recovery," Catherine said.

"What she's trying to say is that we're here for you." Sheila reached for Rowan's hand.

"Excuse me." Rowan set her napkin on her plate and left the room.

"Oh God!" Sheila put her hand to her mouth. "I really bollixed that up. Didn't I?"

"I'll go talk to her." Earl got up.

No one spoke. Catherine fingered the silver band in her ear and Nikki rested a hand on Sheila's shoulder. It was up to Grady to break the silence.

"So, is it always this cloudy in June?"

Earl brought Rowan back ten minutes later.

"Rowan." Sheila stood. "I'm sorry. I…"

"No." Rowan held up her palm. "I'm not feeling up to it, tonight. Sorry to put you through all this trouble."

Grady cast a hungry glance at the abandoned feast and followed his parents out the door.

CHAPTER 6

The next day Grady, Rowan, and Earl checked out of their hotel and boarded the Eurostar train at London's Waterloo Station. They passed through the baggage area by their car's entrance and through the sliding-glass doors that opened into the passenger compartment.

"Uh oh," Earl said.

The overhead storage was not much larger than Rowan's purse and wouldn't hold their violet bags. Muttering, "Excuse me," and, "Pardon," they fought the flow of passengers and went back to the baggage area where they left their suitcases. They returned to the passenger compartment and found their seats. Grady craned his neck and tried to look into the baggage area but couldn't see if anyone was messing with his stuff. He hated that.

A few minutes later the train started to move. Grady stared out the window. Soon the last bits of London receded from view and they were traveling through the countryside. Grady expected the train to pick up speed but it continued at its sluggish pace, passing through shabby train stations that needed a good coat of paint. Bored with the scenery Grady went to the baggage area to get a book out of his case. When no one was looking he scratched his belly, where it had started to chafe under the sweaty money belt, before returning to his seat.

A toddler left his mother and set out on wobbly, stubby legs down the aisle. He stopped amid a group of Japanese ladies in oversized sun hats. The women fussed over the child until his mother called, "Gaspar," and the toddler returned to her lap.

The train slipped into the channel tunnel and all Grady could see through the window was black. He looked instead to Gaspar whose tiny fists were tangled in his mother's long, brown hair. Despite this she maintained her joyful, Madonna-like countenance. Soon the boy grew bored and began his wandering once more. He stopped by Grady and rested a warm, wet hand on Grady's leg.

"How are you?" Rowan stroked the boy's head.

After twenty minutes the train accelerated as it emerged from the tunnel in France. Trees and gleaming buildings whizzed past Grady's window. Gaspar settled his little bottom on the pressed slacks of a thin, African man who entertained the child with stories in French. Eventually the Eurostar slowed as it entered the outskirts of Paris.

"Gaspar." The boy's mother retrieved her son from the African.

Soon dozens of tracks with round-topped European railcars were visible through windows on both sides. The Eurostar entered the station and stopped. They had arrived at Paris's Gare du Nord. Rather than rush for the exits the passengers smiled and wished one another good day in a variety of languages. As Grady left the railcar he looked back at the little boy. From amid the cluster of Japanese ladies, Gaspar turned his blue eyes toward him and grinned.

Grady and his parents rolled their wheeled bags onto the platform and followed the others into the crowded station. Grady had his passport ready but there were no officials waiting to look at it. He compared the time on his watch with that on the giant gilded clock on the wall. No difference.

"The guidebook says the hotel booking service is in the station." Earl looked back and forth. "It must be here somewhere."

While steering his bag through the obstacle course of rushing commuters, Grady stole glances at the steel frames that supported the cavernous structure's dirty glass ceiling. Earl found a bank machine and withdrew some euros. They found the hotel-booking office but a sign on the door stopped them. *Ferme!*

"I told you to make reservations by phone but you wouldn't listen," Rowan snapped.

"Do you know what they charge to make an international call from a hotel?" Earl responded. "We already spent a fortune on that restaurant of yours."

"Guys!" Grady tapped the sign. "It says we can go to the tourist office on the Champs-Elysées."

"We wouldn't have to if your father hadn't been so pig-headed."

"How do we get there?" Grady asked.

"We can take the Metro." Earl fumbled with a map. "We transfer at Les Halles and get off at Franklin Roosevelt. This way." He pointed toward the subway entrance.

As Grady followed his parents the bag he pulled behind him turned turtle and pointed its wheels at the sky.

"Damn!" Grady collapsed the handle and carried his bag. By now his elbow no longer hurt.

Earl bought tickets from a machine and they waited on the

platform. Since neither of his parents was talking, all Grady could do was look at the white tile covering the subway tunnel's curved roof and the billboard with a drawing of a figure in meditation posture that advertised the latest cell phones. Minutes later a rubber-wheeled subway train arrived, and they boarded. Rowan and Earl sat facing away from one another. Both crossed their arms over their chests. The train pulled away.

"*Mesdames et monsieurs.*" A man with long matted hair entered the car and began a long speech in French. After finishing his address he roamed the aisles with a cup to accept donations. Rowan reached for her purse.

"What are you doing?" Earl put a restraining hand on her arm. "Let him get a job like everyone else."

Earl's remark was just another day at the office for the beggar who moved on and eventually went into the next car. Grady and his parents made the transfer and arrived at their destination in a few minutes. At the exit they deposited their tickets into a machine that opened a gate for them to pass. Rowan struggled with her bag on the steps so Earl sighed and carried it for her. They exited onto the Champs-Elysées.

Up the street the Arc de Triomphe stood with proud, tricolor flags flying from the top. Cars whizzed around the traffic circle surrounding the structure. The scene was like a postcard, only real. If only Grady didn't have bag and parents weighing him down, he would have flown like a child's balloon to the monument although he doubted he'd make it through the traffic alive. Rowan lit a cigarette.

"*Pardon mademoiselle,*" she asked a young woman, "*ou est l'office de tourisme?*"

The woman's braids hung to her soft, pink shoulders that her sleeveless blouse left bare. Grady didn't understand her reply but it sure sounded sexy. Following the woman's directions they found the office and booked rooms in Le Fleur Bleu in the Second Arrondissement. Naturally, Earl had chosen the cheapest hotel available. He had to, he said, because the euro was kicking the hell out of the dollar. They returned to the Metro, traveled to the Strassbourg Station, and found the street using Earl's map and compass.

"This doesn't look very savory." Rowan pointed at two black prostitutes who balanced on stiletto heels on the sidewalk.

The two wore low-cut blouses that looked like they'd been sprayed onto their watermelon-sized breasts. As the Evans passed they leered with cash-register eyes but stopped short of a proposition due to Rowan's presence.

The world travelers rolled their bags up and down the street but could not find the hotel. The Middle-Eastern man in a business suit Rowan questioned didn't have a clue either. Neither did the truck driver unloading bread at a café. Finally she asked one of the streetwalkers.

"*Bien sur!*" the woman exclaimed with a huge grin. She let loose a patter of rapid French accompanied by wild gesticulations.

The entrance, it turned out, was hidden around a corner.

"*Votre passports.*" The manager, a fiftyish man with a five o'clock shadow and wrinkled shirt, removed the Galois from the corner of his mouth and examined the Evans's documents. "Ah, you are Americans. You can pay me, tomorrow." He took two keys from under the desk and handed them over.

"Why don't we meet down here in an hour and go to lunch?" Earl said to Grady.

Grady lugged his bag up the narrow staircase to the top floor, opened the flimsy door, and examined his room. With its stained carpet and peeling wallpaper it was the kind of place that suited its clientele. In the bathroom a bar of Le Chat soap from Marseilles preened itself in its wrapper next to the sink. The bed sagged as if a mass-extinction-causing meteor had crashed into the mattress. Grady set down his bag and opened the curtains. He had a balcony. Though pigeon droppings crusted the sooty railing, Grady had a view of the surrounding mansard roofs. On the street below one of the prostitutes had found a customer. Grady smiled. He was in Paris.

Grady returned to the lobby an hour later and found his father waiting.

"Your mother's not coming," Earl said.

"She's not feeling well?" Grady asked.

"She says she's not hungry." Earl jingled the coins in his pocket. "So I guess it's just us two guys. What do you feel like eating?"

"French food?"

"Sounds like a plan."

The prostitutes intercepted them moments after Grady and Earl left.

"*Ça va?*" The taller one batted her eyelashes at Grady after matching his pace.

He shook his head and walked off. She flung curses after him. Grady and Earl walked on, examining menus posted outside restaurants. They entered the Galeries Lafayette shopping mall. The interior was like one of those jeweled Russian Easter eggs. Earl took a picture of the glass dome ceiling. From Grady's vantage point on the lowest level he could see all the floors ending in golden balconies rimmed with wrought-iron railing.

Delights filled the food court – cheeses as big as truck tires, bottles of wine with colorful labels, and pastries. Grady's will to maintain a sensible eating regimen leaked away in dreams of flaky croissants, crème-filled Napoleons, and colorful fruit tarts.

As if immune to these temptations Earl chose a humble, sandwich shop. Using the universal language of pointing and nodding they ordered two of the *croque monsieur* sandwiches displayed in the glass case.

"Maybe I should have tried a *croque madame*," Grady said.

"Leave that to your mother." Earl chose a seat at the counter. It was a little late for lunch so plenty of stools were free.

The clerk heated their sandwiches and brought them over. Since it was Paris, Earl allowed himself a glass of house wine. Grady settled on a Perrier, which earned him a disparaging look from his father.

"I wonder if you can help me out with something." Earl poured wine from a ceramic pitcher into his glass.

Grady, who'd cut a piece from his sandwich, had a mouth too full to answer. He nodded while noting the flavor of ham and melted cheese.

"Don't go worrying your mother with this but we need to keep our spending down," Earl said. "Let her get whatever she wants at restaurants but you and I need to order meals on the inexpensive side. Are you with me?"

Grady swallowed and set down his fork. It took little more than a millisecond for his anger to surface. He had a right to be mad. It wasn't so much the food but the lack of independence. All his friends earned their own money, had cars, and were going off to college while he was stuck in some pseudo childhood. How old did he have to be before his parents stopped telling him what to do? Now he couldn't even order the food he wanted, for Christ's sake!

"Maybe I won't eat anything at all. That way you can save a bundle."

"I'm trying to save so you have something left for college, you idiot."

Grady stared at the man who'd just insulted him. He didn't have to stand for that. "I'm not hungry." Grady stood. "See you later."

"Grady."

His father's call did nothing to slow Grady's rush out of the mall. Ignorant of his anger, shoppers examined tins of truffles and bottles of perfume. Self-satisfied bastards! Fuck them! Fuck them all! Grady half hoped his father would try to stop him. Just let him! Grady would get him in a wristlock, power it with his hips, and cut down so hard Earl would smack his head on the floor. Yeah, let him! Grady shoved open the door and exited onto the Boulevard Haussmann.

"Fucking cheapskate asshole. Thinks he can make me tell his bullshit lies for him," Grady muttered as he walked down the sidewalk. He scratched underneath the money belt. Even his camou pants itched. He hadn't washed them in over a week since it took too long for them to dry hanging on a shower rod.

He traveled several blocks before he realized he was still hungry. He hadn't handled that very well. What would Terry Dobson have done? Retreat? Maybe he hadn't handled it so badly after all.

There on the corner of the bank was a sticker featuring Andre the Giant's face done in totalitarian style under the word "OBEY." Any inclination he had left to post these stickers evaporated. OBEY Giant had obviously gotten here before him. People, he could not communicate with, passed him on the sidewalk. Alone Grady became painfully aware that he didn't speak the language. Being overseas was fantastic until he had to talk to somebody. Then his lack of vocabulary reduced him to the state of an infant. His embarrassment discouraged him from opening his mouth more effectively than a case of lockjaw. He had no desire to return to the hotel so he continued on Boulevard Haussmann reasoning that he wouldn't get lost if he stayed on this street.

After a half hour he found himself once again at the Arc de Triomphe. This time he had no baggage in tow but he still couldn't puzzle out how to cross the traffic and join the tourists swarming over the monument. He debated stepping off the known road but the arch would be an easy landmark. Grady left Boulevard Haussmann and strolled the Champs Elysées, browsing in shop windows for clothing he could never afford. High-fashion women walked past. Someday maybe they'd give him a second look. Soon he entered the Place de la Concorde and crossed the huge square to stand before the Obelisk.

"Whoa!" Grady rested a hand on the wrought-iron fence and stared at the gold hieroglyphics.

Magnificent buildings surrounded him and he could see the Eiffel Tower in the distance. How many of his friends had ever seen anything as cool as this? And he had to go act like a spoiled brat! He shouldn't have smarted off to his dad. Somehow, he'd have to patch things up.

A few customers stood at a hotdog cart nearby. Grady watched the attendant, a woman his age wearing a baggy cloth cap, skewer a baguette on a steel spike, squirt in mustard, and insert a sausage. The price was only a few euros so Grady got in line. When his turn came, Grady held up a finger.

"One, eh *un*."

"Where are you from?" The attendant sliced a baguette in half.

"San Diego, California." An unsightly image popped into Grady's mind as he watched her make like Vlad the Impaler with his bread.

The Paris breeze wafted the faint scent of female sweat to Grady's nostrils. There like tiny keys, the pheromones fit into the locks of his nervous system and freed a complex set of emotions he barely understood.

"Ah California. Is San Diego near San Pedro?" The attendant blew a lock of frizzy, brown hair that had come loose from her cap out of her eyes.

"It's about a hundred miles south, I think. Why are you interested in San Pedro?"

"Do you know the writer Charles Bukowski? He's from there. There's a movie I want to see about him at the Champo." The annoying lock of hair fell into her eyes once again. She tucked it under her cap before placing Grady's sandwich on a paper plate and setting it on the counter. "That'll be three euros."

As Grady took out his wallet, conflicting emotions whirled in his head like wet clothing in a washing machine on the spin cycle. He decided to act.

"That movie sounds interesting. When were you planning to go?"

"Tomorrow maybe." She handed Grady his change.

"Would you like some company?"

"You could meet me here tomorrow afternoon. I'll see if I'm not too tired after work."

Grady ate his hotdog on a bench in a nearby park that was spanned by a grid of gravel paths. Here nature had been tamed to man's ideal of order with lawns formed into neat rectangles and ponds placed in perfect symmetry. Mothers pushed strollers and couples walked hand-in-hand in the sunshine. He finished, tossed his paper in the trash, looked around for a bathroom, and found a small brick building labeled WC. A man in a T-shirt and running shorts entered. Grady was about to follow when a middle-aged woman went in the same doorway.

What the hell? Grady sat and watched. One of the young mothers carried her baby inside. The middle-aged woman left. Had he imagined the man in shorts? Finally another man entered and Grady decided to chance it. If it worked for the locals, it would work for him. Inside he found closed-off stalls and a common area for the sinks.

Feeling more continental after the experience, Grady wandered along the bank of the Seine until he reached the Louvre where a giant glass pyramid squatted amidst the ornate eighteenth-century architecture like an alien spacecraft in *Madame Bovary*. By now the setting sun had formed a half a tablet of baby aspirin on the horizon. It was getting chilly, and even though he'd sooner endure a frozen barium enema, Grady knew he had to return to the hotel and face Earl. He hopped the Metro and was back in twenty minutes.

On the way to his room he met his mother tottering down the stairs in high heels. She was more of a Birkenstock woman and looked out of place in her knee-length black dress and shawl.

"Put a clean shirt on, Grady. We're going to Le Chat Fou."

The cab was already waiting outside when Grady returned to the lobby wearing slacks and a rumpled dress shirt. Rowan fussed with his collar.

"How do you suppose the driver knew where this place was?" Earl held the door.

"Oh Earl!" Rowan slapped him on the shoulder.

After asking their destination the North African driver kept quiet preferring the wail of Arabic music from the speakers to conversation. To Grady's surprise Earl said nothing about their encounter in the mall. Grady felt wary of Earl's silence. He sat up straight expecting a knife thrust to his emotions at any moment.

The driver dropped them off at a restaurant not far from the nightclub. Earl urged salad, escargots, and French onion soup on both him and Rowan. Even though it was delicious, Grady couldn't stop himself from removing the melted cheese from his soup. Several glasses of wine made his parents too jolly to notice.

"Honey bear." Rowan stared into her husband's eyes.

"Baby doll," Earl replied.

Grady wanted to be somewhere else. Rowan excused herself and went to the ladies room.

"Dad, I'm sorry about this afternoon. I..." Grady looked down at his plate and blinked several times to clear his eyes.

"Your mother's illness has been hard on all of us, Grady." Earl rested a hand on his son's shoulder. "Anyway, you were right. This is Paris, home of the best food in the world!" Diners turned their heads at Earl's raised voice. He lowered the volume. "It'd be a goddamn crime not to sample it. We'll pinch pennies somewhere else."

Rowan returned to the table and spread her cloth napkin over her lap.

"You have a smart boy here." Earl put an arm around Grady's shoulders and squeezed, half dragging Grady out of his chair.

"That's what I always told you." Rowan opened the dessert menu. "The pear Belle Hèlene looks good."

Grady and his parents made it into Le Chat Fou moments before the show began. Once they passed the bar in back, an usher directed them to their stadium seats to the left of the stage. Grady looked around. Strangely, there were nearly as many women as men although all appeared to be escorted. Most people wore evening gowns or suits and ties. Embarrassed by his hoody and wrinkled shirt, Grady slouched in his seat.

A woman with blonde hair plaited into cornrows carried a tray through the aisles to deliver drinks. Moments before she reached Earl the lights dimmed and a man in a tuxedo appeared in the spotlight. Judging from the applause he must have been a celebrity but Grady had no clue who he was. The audience punctuated his monolog with laughter but that didn't help either. Rowan, the only one of their party with an understanding of the language, giggled.

"I'll tell you later," she whispered.

The MC finished. A dozen women in bathing suits took the stage and began dancing to a recording of Gloria Gaynor's "I Will Survive." As the chorus line went through their series of kicks and pirouettes, Grady realized the bathing suits were only body paint, and the women's pubic regions had been shaved as smooth as little girls' to maintain the illusion.

He felt a prickling in his armpits, as if the furnace of embarrassment were heating his upper body, and slipped off his hoody. Grady glanced to his right. His parents seemed oblivious. The MC returned and bar girls trolled for drink orders. His parents had cocktails. Grady wasn't thirsty.

A trio of belly dancers came out to shimmy and roll their hips to the rhythm of finger cymbals. For the second time that night Grady heard the off-tune chords of Arabic music. The dancer with black lipstick and blonde pigtails fascinated him. She was tall and somewhat ungainly in her height. While the other two seemed to inhabit their roles, she danced like she didn't belong and was only going through the motions to be a good sport. This appealed to Grady and he felt they were somehow kindred spirits. The women twirled, dropped veils, and exposed their breasts. Again Grady glanced at his parents. From their expressions they could have been watching a Disney movie. Who were these people? Grady had lived with them for eighteen years and realized he didn't know them at all. Soon the dancers removed their remaining clothing. Dark triangles of pubic hair contrasted with white skin in the harsh spotlights as they did back bends to give the audience a closer look.

The final act was a nude woman doing gymnastics on a trapeze while a film projector displayed moving images on her body. After she finished the house lights came on. Grady and his parents joined the crush of people streaming toward the exits. Once outside they walked to a taxi stand to wait for a cab.

"So what did you think of the show, Grady?" Earl asked.

"Very," Grady cleared his throat, "very artistic."

"No architect has ever designed anything more graceful than a woman's body," Earl said.

"Girls that age are so beautiful." Rowan lit a cigarette and took a deep drag. "Then gravity takes over."

"You still look the same as when I met you," Earl said.

To Grady's ear the compliment thunked like a counterfeit coin hitting the pavement but evidently only false currency could buy peace between the sexes. Rowan beamed and kissed Earl's cheek. The cab came and the passengers remained silent on the ride back with Rowan staring wistfully out the window into the Paris night.

Later that night Grady wrestled with dreams of the tall, blonde dancer, her breasts tipped with pink nipples, and her long legs wrapped around him. He woke at 3:00 AM desperate to masturbate but summoned all his internal discipline and rolled over. Tomorrow, he would see the woman from the hotdog stand.

Next morning after a breakfast of croissants and *café au lait*, Grady and his parents went to the Louvre. The famous art museum had once been a castle and Grady viewed its walls in the basement. The displays of ancient Greek, Roman, and Egyptian artifacts on the lower floors occupied them until lunch. The afternoon became a blur but Rowan kept going strong. By 2:00 Grady was feeling the dizzying effects of museum overload. Winged Victory, the Venus de Milo, and the Mona Lisa were the only pieces that made any impression.

"Art's the only thing that lives forever," Rowan said while viewing Leonardo's smaller-than-expected painting. "I wish I'd continued with my music."

"What about the soul?" Earl asked.

Rowan dismissed his question with a snort.

Grady looked at his watch. It was 4:30.

"I've got to go! I'll get my own dinner." He dashed toward the exit.

Grady ran through the Tuileries garden to the Place de la Concorde where he stood panting. He looked around the huge square but the girl and the hotdog stand were gone.

gsankyu@hotmail.com
Dear Marisol,

Can't wait to see you in August. Sorry I haven't written for a while but I've been very busy. We've been in Paris for over a week and are about to move on. All the things you here about the French being rude aren't true, at least not in my experience. The waiters are friendly and many speak English. Oh sure, some people are jerks like that mime at Montmartre when I wouldn't put a coin in his hat.

We've seen most of the sights: the Eiffel Tower, Notre Dame, Louvre, Musée d'Orsay, Rodin Museum, and Napoleon's tomb. The Pompidou Centre was a blast. There was a teacher explaining a Kandinsky painting to a group of seven-year-old kids. My mom dragged us to Jim Morrison's grave at the Père-Lachaise cemetery. A bunch of stoners were lighting candles and playing guitars.

Tomorrow we're taking the high-speed train to Tours where we'll take a look at some chateaus. From there it's on to Nimes, Barcelona, and Madrid. Hope everything is well.

Love,
Grady

OBgrrl@yahoo.com
Dear Grady,

Don't laugh but I got a job at Hotdog Heaven in the mall. You know, the place where they wear the stupid hats. Oh well, it's only for a few months and it will definitely motivate me to get my college degree.

Guess what! Skip Burlow got busted for selling X. His parents hired a big shot lawyer from L.A. but I don't think he's going to get off.

I've saved over $400 so far. At this rate I'll have enough for a plane ticket in another month.

Bye Puffins,
Marisol

gsankyu@hotmail.com
Dear Marisol,

We're in Nimes, France. After Paris we crossed the Pyrenees into Spain and went to Madrid. We've been in Madrid for a week. All the policemen carried machine guns and it seemed like there was a porn stand on every corner. To save money dad made us eat sandwiches at these cafés with hams hanging from the ceiling. I'm sick of ham. I liked the soft drink called horchata. It's made with almonds. Oh, in Spain a tortilla is a potato omelet. I went to Avila when dad took mom to see the doctor for her sore knee. Avila's an old walled city made famous by Saint Theresa. You can still see her mummified finger and stuff. On the way back this guy was waving at me from the museum and yelling, "Santa Teresa! Santa Teresa!" Turned out he was a gay guy who wanted me to go into the confession booth with him. I beat it out of there fast, let me tell you!

From there we swung down to Sevilla and Cordoba. Mom wanted to cross the Med and go to Morocco but dad wouldn't hear of it. Didn't spend much time in

Barcelona. The Gaudi Cathedral is. Signs are in both Spanish (i.e. Castilian) and Catalan. Mom wanted to go to the Dali museum but it was closed.

Anyway Nimes is across the border. Question – what do you do with an old Roman coliseum in a French town? Hold bullfights of course. Mom wouldn't let us go because she thinks it's cruel. But we had paella and sangria in the cafeterias. Go figure! From here we'll follow the Med and eventually head up into Switzerland. I don't know if we're going to Italy. Dad says they're going to have a big transportation strike so we might go north through Germany instead. I'll keep you posted.

God, I miss you!

Grady

PS I didn't mention that mom's OK. Her leg's sore but he doctor gave her some anti-inflammatories and told her to take it easy a bit.

OBgrrl@yahoo.com

Dear Grady,

Glad to hear you mom's OK. I'm bummed about Italy, though. I was really looking forward to Florence. Oh well, what's there to see in Germany? My mom's been giving me a hard time about going. She says I should save my money for college but don't worry. I'll bring her around. The sooner you sort out your plans the better. Once I buy my ticket, she'll have to let me go.

Bye Puffins,

Marisol

CHAPTER 7

A cab dropped them off at a dock in an industrial zone of northeast Strasbourg. Rowan climbed out of the backseat and refused Grady's offer of help. She was moving better than she had a few days earlier but still favored her sore knee. If all went according to plan, the Rhine cruise would give it time to heal and she'd be better when they reached Amsterdam.

Their boat, the four-hundred-foot Beethoven, resembled the stretch limos Grady had seen in San Diego. Instead of elongating an SUV or pickup truck to ridiculous lengths, the builders of the Beethoven had stretched a cabin cruiser.

Grady walked by Rowan's side as she limped toward the gangway. Carrying two bags and their itinerary Earl trudged behind. They caught up with the other passengers inching toward the hatch. When they reached the middle of the gangway, a gust of wind snatched the itinerary from Earl's fingers.

"Shit!" He put down the suitcases.

A thin man in a baseball cap and aviator glasses stopped the runaway paper with a deft stomp of his purplish-white running shoe.

"Here you go." He handed the itinerary back to Earl.

"Thanks." Earl shook hands. "I'm Earl Evans. This is my wife, Rowan, and son, Grady."

"Pleased to meet you. I'm Dick Klausen and this is my wife, Maria."

Dick Klausen was clean-shaven and had a prominent chin. He wore khaki slacks and a blue nylon jacket. From his salt-and-pepper hair, Grady guessed he was in his early forties. Maria was a tall woman with a tiny waist, ample breasts, and sun-damaged skin tanned to the reddish brown of an old leather sofa, the same color as her hair. She wore a pastel blue sweater and a pair of white shorts.

"How do you do?" Maria said.

"So, where are you from?" Dick asked.

"San Diego."

"Californicators, huh?" Dick scratched his chin. "We're from Detroit. What line of work are you in, Earl?"

"Defense contracting. You?"

"I'm a stockbroker."

By now they'd reached to top of the gangway. Earl bid goodbye to the Klausens and handed his tickets to the purser who assigned a crewman to take their bags. Because the pricey cabins were too small for three, Earl had booked Grady into one that he would have to share with a stranger.

"Think of it as a learning experience," Earl had said. "You'll get to know someone from another culture."

Grady thanked the crewman for carrying his bag, opened the door to his quarters, and was nearly bowled over by the stench of sweat. The smell was more than unpleasant. It was painful as if the billions of odor molecules jabbed the sensitive tissues of his nostrils with microscopic needles. The source of this olfactory assault was a tall man speaking a Slavic language into a cell phone. His white muscle shirt revealed a weightlifter's upper torso and his dirty-blonde hair had been styled into a no-nonsense brush cut. He nodded to Grady from where he slouched by the window and returned to his conversation.

Grady set his suitcase down. When his roommate hung up, he decided to introduce himself.

"Hi, I'm Grady."

"Bogdan." The roommate clasped Grady's proffered hand with a bone-crushing grip.

"Where are you from?" By pressing his index and middle fingers against the inside of Bogdan's wrist, Grady neutralized the pressure of Bogdan's grasp. Score one for brains over brute strength!

Bogdan shrugged his massive shoulders. He didn't speak English. Grady heard the low rumble of the boat's diesel motors turning over and felt a lurch as they got under way. He looked at his watch. It was almost time for dinner. Grady motioned that he was leaving. Bogdan nodded and dialed another number.

The spacious dining room was located on the top deck where diners could watch scenery through the large windows. For the time being there were only barges and chemical plants. Grady took his assigned seat under a chandelier. His parents and two other couples were already seated.

"*Konbanwa.*" He repeated one of the simple phrases he knew to the Japanese on Rowan's left. Both smiled and nodded their heads.

"How's your room?" Rowan asked.

"My roommate has a serious B.O. problem." Grady sat down and spread a napkin on his lap.

"Now Grady, sometimes we have to make allowances for people from other cultures." Rowan nibbled a slice of bread and blotted her mouth with a napkin.

"It's worse than teargas, mom."

"If it's that awful, you shouldn't have to put up with it," Rowan said.

"I'll talk to the purser," Earl said but nothing would come of it.

"Hey Earl! How're you doing?" Dick Klausen slapped Grady's father on the back. "Rowan. Grady."

His wife, Maria, had changed into a pastel, terrycloth dress.

"Good, Dick. And you?"

"Couldn't be better!" Dick turned to the Japanese. "Say buddy, do you mind trading places with us so we can eat with our pals Earl and Rowan?"

The Japanese pointed to the seat numbers on his tickets.

"Yes, yes. You can sit at that table over there with a delightful Dutch couple." Dick pointed across the room and half dragged the Japanese out of their seats. "That's better." Dick held the chair for Maria and sat next to her. "So where are you headed after Amsterdam, Earl?"

"We're traveling around the world."

"You don't say. I hope you're not planning on the Middle East."

A waiter interrupted to take drink orders. Earl chose German beer. Dick and Maria ordered screwdrivers.

"You were saying about the Middle East?"

"I'd stay away from there if I were you," Dick said. "The whole Iraq nuke thing is just the tip of the iceberg, my friend. The tip of the iceberg."

"Dick has contacts at the CIA," Maria said.

"You don't say."

The waiter brought their drinks.

"Some heavy shit's gonna go down in that part of the world, believe you me." Dick stirred his drink with a swizzle stick and took a gulp. "What I'm about to tell you is in the strictest confidence." He looked over his shoulder, turned back, and lowered his voice. "In the 1920s a British archeologist found a crystal skull near the Maya ruins at Tulum. Our scientists examined it under the microscope and found no chisel marks, which means it couldn't have been made by human beings with ancient technology."

"No shit," Grady said.

"It gets better," Dick said to Grady. "When they shined a laser through it, it projected a hologram that contains partial plans for some fascinating technology. I'm talking about faster-than-light space travel, unlimited pollution-free energy, and even immortality."

The other couple at the table turned away from Dick and began conversing in German.

"Tell them about the other skulls, Dick," Maria said.

"The aliens left crystal skulls at the sites of all ancient civilizations – Mexico, Peru, Greece, Egypt, and so on. To get a complete set of plans you need to collect all of them. Why do you think we're interested in Iraq? It isn't for oil, my friend. Saddam Hussein has the skull from Babylon. Why do you think we send billions of dollars to Israel? Because the Mossad knows where two of the skulls are located."

A waiter brought salads of bib lettuce and pickled vegetables.

"The CIA's number-one priority is to get control of those skulls before the Iranians do. Of course, you have the Russian Mafia in the mix too. It's so vital to the national interest that the president would rather risk nuclear war than let those skulls fall into the ayatollahs' hands."

"Dick tells people how to protect their assets from the coming apocalypse," Maria said.

"You don't say."

"Precious metals, Earl." Dick spoke with his mouth full and waved his fork with a piece of lettuce still stuck to the tines for emphasis. "Precious metals."

The waiter brought dinner plates heaped with sausages, red cabbage, and spaetzels. Grady wolfed down his food and left the table before dessert. As Grady walked away, Dick was still haranguing his parents with conspiracy theories and bogus investment advice. The computers were available. Grady paid the attendant and checked his e-mail.

OBgrrl@yahoo.com
Dear Grady,
There's no way to say this except to come right out with it. I can't go to

Europe this summer. The scholarship I was counting on fell through so I'll need to use the money I earned for school.

Try not to be too disappointed, darling. The ten months you have left will pass quickly. Before you know it, we'll be together again.

I hope your mom is doing well. I miss you.

Bye Puffins,

Marisol

Grady closed the e-mail and stared at some news site while registering nothing. Sometime during the hour he spent on the Internet, the Beethoven tied up in Karlsruhe. The sun had already gone down when Grady returned to his cabin. Bogdan wasn't there. Grady got his hopes up that he wouldn't return, turned down the foldout bed, and got under the covers. He lay there looking out the window at the lights across the river. His thoughts turned to how Marisol had been almost within reach until she changed her mind.

Grady drifted into an uneasy sleep and dreamed that a turbaned ayatollah chased him with a machete. The sound of a key in the lock woke him. Bogdan entered like a locomotive dragging two hundred boxcars of stench. Though he moved carefully about the cabin, his attempts at quiet only irritated Grady all the more. Rather than interact Grady feigned sleep. He lay still for what he judged the minimum amount of time that wouldn't hurt his roommate's feelings. Then around 5:00 AM he dressed and got the hell out of there.

The lounge was deserted. Grady sat on a couch near the window. Breakfast wouldn't be for another hour. There was nothing to do but look out into the gray morning. In the distance a car approached a warehouse. The driver killed the headlights and went inside. Then all was still. Exhaustion clung to Grady like heavy clothes to a drowning man. He lacked the strength to lift his limbs and felt an overwhelming urge to strip off his socks. He closed his eyes.

Grady felt like he was falling and jerked himself awake. The sounds of the crew's conversation in German came from the neighboring room. Grady checked his watch. It was time for breakfast. He nodded between sleep and consciousness for over an hour.

"Grady! What are you doing here at this hour?"

Grady sat up, wiped the drool from the corner of his mouth, and looked at his mother who stood by the couch wearing powder-blue sweatpants and a cotton top. His skin felt greasy and his mouth tasted as if he'd been swilling stale coffee and vinegar.

"Couldn't sleep," he said.

"You look terrible." Rowan reached into her purse and withdrew the cabin key. "Here. Why don't you go take a nap in our room?"

"I'll get breakfast first. Where's dad?"

"Still asleep." Rowan sat and sank into the cushions next to her son to wait for the dining room to open. "I hope that nut case won't be at our table. I've just about had enough of his stupid ideas."

"Marisol's not coming, mom."

"Oh Grady, I'm sorry."

"She says she has to save money for tuition."

"This cruise hasn't worked out too well for you. Has it?" Rowan shook her head. "Well, maybe she can come this Christmas."

"You think she's trying to dump me?"

"I think it's hard to have a relationship when you're thousands of miles apart," Rowan said, "especially when you're eighteen."

"It's just not worth it."

"What's not, Grady?"

"Girls, romance, whatever."

"You don't know that it won't work out. Besides you don't love someone because of some dream future you might get to. You love them because you love them."

Grady scratched his head. His mother might as well have been reciting the *Nag Hammadi* in Aramaic.

"It's like your heart's a warrior suited up for battle," Rowan continued. "If it hides behind a rock, the Morlocks will take over the world. So kick the horse with your spurs and charge! Don't let the Morlocks win, Grady."

Even if she just didn't get it, it was hard not to laugh when his mother got worked up. The staff opened the dining room and several waiting passengers entered.

"Let's get something to eat." Grady xescorted his mother inside.

Dick and Maria Klausen were already seated when Grady and Rowan arrived at the table. Dick looked up, preventing Grady from fleeing unobserved.

"Morning! How'd you sleep?" the Detroit blowhard asked.

"Coffee," Grady mumbled.

Maria passed the coffeepot. Grady stuffed himself with bread, cold cuts, and cheese to fight the fatigue while Dick talked about Roswell.

"You ever think about what you want to do after college?" Dick asked.

Grady shook his head.

"One word – plastics."

Grady stared. Dick and Maria broke into guffaws.

"Just kidding, kid." Dick spread marmalade on his toast. "You never seen that movie? Seriously if I were you, I'd go into law. With everybody suing everybody else there's plenty of work to go around."

"Morning." Earl yawned and sat down.

Grady excused himself, stumbled off to his parents' cabin, and slept for several hours. He woke in the afternoon, having missed the ninety-minute stop at Speyer to see the Romanesque cathedral. He took a shower, changed back into his dirty clothes, and headed to the lounge for a beer and some snacks. Unlike earlier that morning it was crowded with passengers and boisterous conversation. Grady ordered at the bar.

"So, are you traveling with that man and his wife?" a cherubic man, Grady recognized from the dining room asked with a German accent. Despite a bald spot on his head, the man's plump face and rosy cheeks radiated youth and good humor.

"You mean the stock broker?" Grady asked.

The man nodded.

"Hell no! My parents and I met him on the boat, and now we can't get rid of him."

The stranger nodded as if in approval. "I'm Dieter and this is my wife Susanna." The woman stood roughly a head taller than him. The hair on her head was darker than her eyebrows, and a half-dozen silver studs and rings occupied the piercings in her right ear. "We were thinking of going to the upper deck. Perhaps you'd like to join us."

"Okay." Grady followed them outside.

The deck was less crowded than the lounge and despite the hum of diesel engines quieter as well. Hills crowded both sides of the river like sleeping guard dogs. They found three unoccupied deck chairs behind the boat's superstructure. Once he was out of the wind, the sun warmed Grady's skin.

"Where are you from?" Susanna asked.

"San Diego, California."

"Ah, where the weather is always perfect," Dieter said. "I went to college at USC."

"My father wouldn't let me go to America," Susanna said. "He was a socialist and didn't approve of your president."

"Oh." The beer on Grady's empty stomach was making him light headed. "So, are you German?"

"Swiss." Dieter didn't seem to take offence. "From Zurich. Have you visited Switzerland on your journeys?"

Grady nodded. "I really liked Bern. They had bears, great chocolate, and people were riding inner tubes in the river. We saw Geneva and Lugano too."

"You really should see the Interlaken." Susanna pronounced the th as d.

"Maybe we will. We're circling the world." Grady abandoned his normal reticence. "My mom wants to travel while she still can. Cancer."

"Ah." Dieter rested a hand on Grady's shoulder for a moment. Then his eyes took on a demented gleam. "This friend of yours with the crystal skulls, do you think he really believes it?"

"Hard to say," Grady said.

"I propose we perform a little experiment to find out."

The Klausens were already pestering Grady's parents when he joined them at the lunch table.

"If it weren't for the British, we'd have a working missile defense by now," Dick said.

"Why is that, Dick?" Earl turned his tired eyes to the nuisance.

"Because of the anti-Semitic Zionists."

"Anti-Semitic Zionists!" Grady looked at Dick wide-eyed. "Isn't that a contradiction in terms?"

"It has to do with the Death Cult of Isis," Dick said.

"Death Cult of Isis!" Earl snorted.

"It's not a joke, you know!" Dick's face flushed. He stood, tossed his napkin on the table, and followed by Maria walked off.

"It's not a joke, you know," Earl mocked.

Everyone at the table, including the German couple, laughed. Grady realized it was time to let his parents in on the plan.

That afternoon his father loitered near the phones with Grady stationed several feet away as lookout. Sooner or later Dick and Maria would have to walk by. Fortunately Grady only had to wait a half hour before he spotted them.

"Mr. Klausen," he said loudly enough to be heard by Earl. "I'm sorry about my dad. He's been under a lot of stress lately. When you get some time, I'd love to hear more about the British."

"Of course, Grady. Maybe at dinner." Dick and his wife continued on their way.

Earl played his part as if he'd grown up in the theater. When Dick got within earshot he bellowed into the phone, "Look, I don't care what Langley says. If you don't get me that money by tonight, the Elf will sell the package to the Russian mob." He hung up and walked away leaving behind a picture of a crystal skull that Grady had printed off the Internet.

In the evening the Beethoven tied up at Rüdesheim. A few passengers chose to eat in town but Grady and his parents stayed on board as did Dick and Maria. As usual Dick monopolized the dinner conversation with talk of pyramids and UFO cover ups. After the waiter brought apricot strudel for dessert Earl turned to Rowan.

"Can you and Grady get by on your own in Amsterdam for a few days? I need to take a quick trip to Saudi."

"Damn it, Earl! This was supposed to be our vacation!"

"I can't get out of it. Dr. Krueger is having difficulties at the refinery."

"That's what you always say." Rowan faked a sulk while Grady looked at his plate to avoid busting up. "If it isn't the refinery in Arabia, it's the coffee plantation in Pakistan or the resort in Thailand. Well mister, you just go ahead but don't count on us being there when you get back."

When Grady and Rowan disembarked from the Beethoven that night, Earl was already at the bottom of the gangway with Dieter. As soon as Dick came into view, Earl raised his voice.

"Look, I'll get the money! Just give me a few more days!"

Dieter muttered something, Grady couldn't hear, and Earl returned to the boat.

"Dad!" Grady called as his father rushed past. "Aren't you coming?"

Meanwhile Dieter opened a map and began walking off toward

the remains of the city's Fifteenth Century fortifications. When the Klausens got to the bottom of the gangway, Dick bent over and pretended to tie his shoe.

"Dick, aren't you coming to the Drosselgasse?" Grady asked.

"I want to see the Eagles' Tower first. I'll catch up with you."

"Let's get going before they change their minds," Rowan muttered under her breath. She and Grady made their escape.

After a short walk Grady and his mom joined the throngs of tourists crowding the ten-foot-wide alley. There were too many people break out of the pack and stride ahead so they matched the crowd's plodding pace and looked at the half-timbered buildings and hanging wooden placards. Walking single file made conversation impossible and even if they'd walked side by side, the din of oompah bands coming from beer gardens and *weinstubes* would have made in difficult to hear.

They found a reasonably priced wine bar where a waiter with a black leather money pouch brought them glasses of an excellent local Riesling. Rowan's knee was still sore so she returned to the boat leaving Grady behind. He had no desire to go back to his cabin so he wandered the Drosselgasse eventually settling in a nightclub that featured a reggae band. Grady wondered how he had gotten by so long without watching teens with blonde dreadlocks mouthing the words of Bob Marley in fake Jamaican accents. When Grady returned to the Beethoven after midnight, he spied Dieter carrying a stuffed pillowcase on board and Dick Klausen watching from the shadows.

Dick's suspicion grew toxic when Earl didn't show up for breakfast the next morning.

"Where's your husband?" he asked Rowan.

"Oh uh." She paused as if fighting back Betty Davis tears. "He's not feeling well. Excuse me." She left clutching the napkin to her eyes.

The Beethoven entered the Rhine Gorge, a fairytale landscape of castles and villages. Even the hardcore drinkers, who'd spent the entire cruise in an alcoholic stupor, came out on deck to view the castles clinging to impossibly steep crags like desperate mountain climbers. The scenery stimulated Grady's imagination. He daydreamed about chivalry based mostly on old movies he'd seen on TV – Ivanhoe, Arthur, and Robin Hood. He pictured himself dressed in a golden tunic while performing his vigil in a chapel before being dubbed Sir Grady by the king. Gleaming armor, a solid steed, and riding into battle with a token of a lady's favor tied to his lance. Were German knights the same as the English? The boat chugged past the Lorelei Cliff where sirens were rumored to lure sailors to their deaths on the rocks below.

That night the Beethoven docked at Koenigswinter and Earl made a show of limping down the gangway supported by his wife. Instead of pursuing the Evans into town like a cloud of gnats, Dick and Maria stayed behind to keep an eye on Dieter and his strange cargo.

The next morning the Beethoven cruised to Cologne and tied up for a few hours so its passengers could visit the famous cathedral. There Dieter met a bearded man at the bottom of the gangway. The leather jacket and wraparound sunglasses the stranger wore gave him an air of mystery. The two men hurried away from the rest of the passengers and traded the pillowcase for an envelope. When Dick saw the stranger walking away with the pillowcase, his eyes took on a look of panic. He mumbled a few quick words to Maria and set off in pursuit.

When Grady and his parents returned to the boat hours later, Maria waited, perched on their two suitcases on the dock but Dick Klausen was nowhere to be seen. She remained there when the Beethoven pulled away.

Still reluctant after their experience with Sheila, Grady's parents met Dieter and Susanna afterwards in the lounge. Earl bought a round of beers.

"What a great scam!"

"I can't get over the look on his wife's face." Rowan doubled over laughing.

"What was in the bag, anyway?" Grady asked.

"Oh, an Emmentaler cheese," Dieter said. "My cousin asked me to bring him one from Zurich."

CHAPTER 8

"I don't care what the guidebook says." Rowan crossed her arms over her chest. "I'm not getting on another boat."

They sat in the living room of the hotel suite not far from Amsterdam's Dam Square. A mural depicting a bread loaf wearing a cook's hat decorated the wall. The whole-wheat chef was kneading a ball of dough into the shape of a woman.

"But the guidebook says a canal cruise is the best way to see Amsterdam," Earl said. "And you don't want to overdo it with your knee."

"My knee's fine, Earl."

"How about a Segway tour?" Grady held up a violet flier he'd picked up at the dock when they'd disembarked from the Beethoven. "They have them day and night."

"Would you both please stop it? My knee is fine! Now, I need to get ready to go to the Rijksmuseum." Rowan limped into the bathroom to put on her makeup. She came out with her head bent to a hand that was inserting an earring.

Grady looked at his mother's face. The sunlight made the contrast between rouge and foundation as obvious as a coastline seen from a geo-synchronous satellite. Why did women do this to themselves? Grady met Earl's eyes and for a brief moment the two men shared a common understanding.

"Oh Grady, I talked to the desk clerk. She says there's an aikido dojo not far from here." Rowan ducked into a bedroom and returned with a Xeroxed map with the route to the dojo traced in yellow magic marker. "Maybe you'd like to stop in."

As well as Rembrandt's *Night Watch*, displayed behind bulletproof glass, the Rijksmuseum had the stern of a captured English sailing ship and a great collection of Japanese swords. The latter came about because Holland was one of the few nations allowed to trade with Japan during the Tokugawa era. Grady paused in front of the bug-like samurai armor. It was made of red lacquer and consisted of a horned, flanged helmet, face guard bristling with horsehair mustache, chest guard, shin guards, gloves, and densely-woven shoulder and groin protectors. His parents had to pull him away.

Rowan was too tired to take in the Van Gogh Museum so they had *rijsttafel* for a late lunch at an Indonesian restaurant. The waiter set a seemingly endless supply dishes on the table – chicken *satay* on bamboo skewers, fiery *sambals*, fish curry, and meat in peanut sauce. Grady kept eating long after common sense told him to quit and left the restaurant feeling as if he were hauling a load of concrete blocks in his gut. He'd never digest before that night's aikido class but the sight of the samurai weapons in the museum inspired him to go anyway.

When they got back to the hotel, Grady stripped off his money belt and scratched his sweaty belly. He felt safer leaving his passport behind than taking it to the dojo. In the months he'd worn it, the garment had developed a serious funk. Grady swore he'd wash it in the sink when he got back. He unpacked his suitcase to dig out his lightweight karate gi. Of course, it was on the bottom forcing him to remove everything else he'd packed. Packing! Unpacking! What a pain! He'd be glad when he didn't have to live out of a suitcase anymore. Grady clambered down the stairs and set out on foot toward the dojo. After a fifteen-minute walk he ended up in front of a narrow, multistory house. The door handle at the top of the stairs would not turn. He looked back and forth. A dark-haired woman was unchaining a bicycle from a railing two doors down.

"Aikido dojo?" Grady pointed at the locked door.

"They moved six months ago." The thin woman wore thick eyeliner that had smudged on the pale skin surrounding her eyes.

"But I came all the way from America." Grady set his gi down on the steps.

"Hold on." The woman dialed her cell phone and spoke in rapid-fire Dutch. "Their new place is north of the Vondelpark. They say they're looking forward to meeting you. Do you have a map?"

Grady showed her his Xeroxed map.

"You can get on the number-one tram on the Leidsegracht and get off on Overtoom here." She stabbed her finger at the paper. "It's only a short walk after that."

"Thanks."

"You're welcome." She got on her bicycle and rode off sounding the bell.

Grady looked at his watch. He had fifteen minutes before the start of class. Ordinarily he would just try another time but the bicycle woman had told them he was coming so he couldn't back out. Grady double-timed it to Leidsegracht and stood by the tracks tapping his foot against the pavement until the tram arrived.

"Vondelpark?" he asked.

The driver nodded. In his rush Grady had cut in front of a woman hauling two bulging plastic bags. He boarded and fumbled in his pocket for change to pay the ticket. Once on board the woman with the bags collapsed panting in the seat behind his. The tram crossed picturesque canals but Grady was too stressed to admire the green water and trendy shops. As always whenever he was late, he felt the need to urinate. Each time the tram stopped to pick up or let off passengers, Grady looked at his watch. Finally the driver stopped at Grady's exit.

"Vondelpark."

Grady pushed the button to open the door, darted in front of the other exiting passengers, and hustled to his destination. By the time he got to the dojo, nervous sweat permeated his shirt. He entered and placed his shoes next to the sandals and sneakers lined up like soldiers on the wooden rack by the door.

"*Ichi, ni, san, shi, ...*" sounded the instructor's voice counting warm up exercises from the mat.

Grady ducked into the men's changing room where mercifully he found a toilet. He struggled into his gi, left his street clothes hanging on a wooden peg, hurried to kneel at the edge of the pale green *tatami*. There he waited for the instructor's permission to join class.

The instructor intercepted his opponent's downward strike, made a circle with the man's elbow forcing him to bend at the waist, and took him to the mat. The teacher's potbelly made his black *hakama* hang awkwardly from his frame but it no doubt lowered his center of gravity and gave him a base as solid as a tree stump's. He was in his early forties, had a brushy mustache, and wore his thinning ginger hair long so it flopped whenever his did a spinning technique. He finished demonstrating the *shomenuchi ikkyo* and nodded to Grady who bowed, stepped on the mat, and found a partner.

At first Grady's technique was awkward from lack of practice but he soon got into the groove. As his opponent raised his arm, Grady entered and caught it before the downward motion began. Soon Grady's *ikkyo* smoothed out and he even remembered to spiral the arm into his opponent's body to further destroy his balance. The instructor clapped his hands. Grady bowed and joined the others kneeling. The instructor pointed to Grady who rose and stood ready to attack.

"Collar grab," the teacher said.

As Grady stepped forward and extended his arm, a slap knocked his head to the right. Somehow he managed to get a grip on the instructor's lapel but Grady's reward was a blinding pain in his wrist. Grady buckled his knees under the influence of the teacher's powerful *nikyo* and found himself face down. The instructor's pin nearly tore Grady's shoulder out of its socket. He pounded the mat in submission. The teacher held the pin for an agonizing second before letting up. Grady got to his feet.

"You block next time, eh?" The teacher pointed to his lapel, and Grady lunged for it once more.

Grady stopped the strike but the teacher grabbed the blocking hand and cranked the wrist. Grady pivoted and collapsed into an awkward heap on the mat. Damn it! Didn't that idiot know he couldn't do a break fall? Something was torn in Grady's wrist. The instructor clapped. Grady bowed and went to practice with the others.

By babying his throbbing wrist, Grady made it through the rest of the class without further injury. Spending the second half working on *suwariwaza* helped. Grady skinned his knees on these kneeling techniques but they would heal. The class ended without the teacher calling Grady up to *uke* again. After they bowed out, Grady limped to the changing room.

"We work out every night," Grady's first partner said. "Will we see you, tomorrow?"

"I don't know." Grady stepped into his pants. The fingers of his injured hand could not grip the zipper. "We'll just be in Amsterdam for a few days."

"Have you checked out the Red Light District and the coffee shops?" asked a dark-haired man whose mustache seemed to be a carbon copy of the teacher's.

"No, just the Rijksmuseum."

"It wouldn't be a trip to Amsterdam if you didn't party."

The smell at the tram stop reminded Grady of burning leaves. Of course, cannabis! He looked around and spotted a woman in shorts and Ugg boots passing a joint to a bearded man at a table out front of a coffee shop. The façade was painted a deep, glossy green with "Urban Ecstasy" stenciled in white over the plate glass window.

Grady stepped inside and stood by the door. A dozen patrons lounged with joints in the small, dimly lit space while hip-hop played from the speakers. Grady felt like the new kid in gym class who didn't know the rules to the ball game everyone was playing. Unable to summon the courage to go farther he turned and left.

On the ride back to the hotel he cradled his hurt hand in a bag of crushed ice he'd gotten at a French fry stand. When he got back to the suite, his parents were gone. With nothing else to do Grady washed his money belt in the sink and hung it to dry. He showered, watched TV, and waited for them to return. They still weren't back by 11:00 so he went to bed.

The sound of the door opening woke him. He heard giggling and the sound of something falling off the table.

"Shit!" Earl said.

"Shh, you'll wake him." More giggling.

Grady turned over.

Grady woke at 2:00 AM and couldn't get back to sleep so he went to the living room to watch TV. After cycling through several channels he stopped on a French station showing softcore porn and turned the sound down so his parents wouldn't hear. Of course, the couples were beautiful and athletic. The camera caught them demonstrating gymnastic sex without showing anything wet or hairy. The image of a woman with chestnut hair lying naked atop her lover while holding him with both arms and thighs stuck in Grady's mind. Thinking how nice that would be Grady turned off the television and went back to bed.

Why shouldn't he get laid while he had a chance? Marisol renounced all claims on him when she backed out of her planned visit and it would be another ten months before he got back, anyway. It was all legal and easy here. Why not put some of the money from selling his Volvo to good use? At least he could take a look.

Next afternoon he and his parents returned to their suite after visiting the Anne Frank House and finally taking the canal cruise. Grady brushed his teeth and headed for the door.

"I'm going to aikido, mom."

"Don't you need your gi?"

"At the Dutch dojos they have clean ones you can borrow."

"Oh." Rowan turned back to her magazine. "Have a good time."

Even before dark, the Red Light District was crowded but it was a mixed crowd. As well as testosterone-fueled lads with short hair swaggering and leering there were tour groups led by women carrying flags. Trying to look inconspicuous Grady joined one of these and followed them into the narrow alleyways near the Old Church. There real, flesh and blood women in panties and bras posed behind black-framed picture windows.

His pace slowed by the tourists, Grady looked without being obvious. Red, neon lights were mounted horizontally over each window and no-photography signs were everywhere. The women were gorgeous often with blonde hair, outstanding figures, and skin the color of honey. A few leaned out of doorways to smoke.

Bolder now, Grady abandoned the tour group to explore on his own. He passed several Irish bars on his way toward the church. The women there were older with torn nylons and rolls of fat bulging from panties. Grady guessed they were probably cheaper too. He crossed a bridge and passed sex shops without looking inside and wondered why they had to make sex crass and stupid.

He smelled marijuana smoke, spotted a coffee shop, and ducked inside. In the back a few people sat smoking joints at tables with candles and ash trays. Grady abandoned any reservations he'd had. What the hell? He'd probably never be anywhere else where marijuana was legal. He looked around to see where he should go. There were two counters, one by the door and another farther inside with cups and a coffee maker. He approached the former.

"Do you have anything local?"

"*Nederwiet?* We have three" The clerk, a man with a crew cut, brought out three plastic containers and let Grady smell each. "This one was runner up in last year's *High Times* contest."

Grady chose the one with the most floral fragrance. If he had wanted, he could have examined the buds under the magnifying glass mounted on the counter but he wouldn't have known what to look for.

"That'll be twelve euros a gram." The clerk handed Grady a plastic bag of dope the size of a quarter and pointed to a shelf. "Papers are over there."

Grady paid with a twenty, his change adding to the cumbersome mass of coins in his pockets. He found a chair in the back and set about rolling a joint, which proved more difficult than he thought. The papers were thin, his hand still hurt, and the buds tended to clump together.

"You want something to drink?" asked the waitress in a low-cut sweatshirt that revealed beautiful shoulders and a black bra strap. Tribal tattoos decorated her forearms.

"An orange juice." Grady lit the joint from a candle and took a toke.

He held his breath, exhaled, took another hit, and found that the joint had gone out. Feeling sheepish he relit it and looked around the room to see if others were mocking him for his ineptness. The Asian guy slumped in the corner with a white girlfriend stared in Grady's direction with unfocused eyes.

"Three euros." The waitress set the juice on Grady's table.

He paid with a five-euro bill adding even more change to his bulging pocket. Grady relit the joint and took another toke. The staring guy was still looking at him. After studying him, Grady decided the guy was staring because he was simply stoned. It wasn't Grady at all. A new guy walked in with slow, controlled movements much like a drunk driver doing twenty miles per hour below the speed limit. Grady kept smoking and eventually the weed kicked in. His head felt as if it descended in a diving bell to the bottom of a carbonated ocean. Bubbles formed around the bass notes of the reggae on the stereo, rose up his spine, and popped red and violet flashes in his consciousness. Grady finished the joint. The fizzing in his brain got louder until it sounded like a rain of ball bearings on sheet metal. Coming from a country where marijuana is illegal he felt an almost paranoid need not to show how stoned he was. He sipped his juice in a false show of control but it was no good. Nearby people he was previously unaware of seemed to materialize next to him as if playing a prank. His tiny voice of remaining reason told him it was not a trick but simply the fact that the marijuana had narrowed his perception. He was clearly messed up, too messed up to go outside and deal with pickpockets, propositions, and con games. The coffee shop was an island of safety that he wouldn't leave. He'd sit right here under the coconut tree.

There was nothing to do but relax and go with it. He got the sense that nothing mattered. Neither his mother's cancer nor his worries about college were important. He constantly forgot his train of thought allowing his mind put together different concepts in seemingly profound ways. Maybe he should write it all down but since nothing mattered, he didn't. A British guy sat with a joint at the counter and chatted up the waitress. She smiled and talked about her trip to the city of Bath. Grady wanted to mention that he'd just been there but again nothing mattered.

It took a few hours before he felt clear enough to leave. The women were still in the windows and due to his residual intoxication he felt more comfortable looking. A few doors from the coffee shop one woman caught his attention. Her body looked like a cheerleader's but her face stayed with him. Smiling and wearing rectangular wire-rimmed glasses, she somehow seemed human and sincere. Momentum carried Grady past her but on the way home he categorized the sex workers into three types, the ugly ones, the porn producer's wet dreams, and the rare few who seemed both beautiful and sincere.

The walk back to the apartment finished clearing his head. Once in the building he trudged up the stairs, inserted the key, and eased the door open. It was dark inside. He was home free. Grady fumbled out of his shoes. The light came on.

"Mom!"

"How was aikido?" Rowan wore the oversized Hello Kitty T-shirt she usually slept in. She walked past the entryway and into the kitchen.

"Pretty good." Grady heard her rattling bowls in the cupboard. "I went out with some of the guys from the dojo afterwards." He sniffed his shirt to see if it smelled like marijuana smoke.

The refrigerator door clunked. Rowan carried two bowls and a half-liter of Cherry Garcia ice cream into the living room, set them on the coffee table beside the paperback copy of Sylvia Plath's *Ariel*, and curled up on the couch.

"Where's dad?"

"Asleep." Rowan filled the bowls and handed Grady one.

Terrified to expose his bloodshot eyes, Grady focused on the ice cream with the concentration of a Zen master, finished in less than a minute, and stood to escape.

"Well, guess I'll go to bed too."

"Don't go. We hardly get to spend time together anymore," Rowan said when he was halfway to the kitchen.

With her legs tucked under the tent of her T-shirt his mother looked vulnerable as a little girl.

"Okay." Grady returned and bent his spoon chipping a jagged hunk of ice cream from the container.

"Let's see what's on TV." Rowan picked up the remote and flipped through the channels including three Dutch stations, a few in French, CNN, BBC news, and one in German.

Eventually she settled on a British sitcom called Father Ted. From what Grady could tell the episode involved a plot to murder contestants in a sheep beauty contest and a drunken priest whose every other word was, "arse."

"You ever miss it?" Grady asked. "Being in a band?"

"Oh, Grady." Rowan took a breath. "It was fun for a while. We played all the best places in DC: the Psychedelly, the 9:30 Club. Even opened for the Dead Kennedys but the skinheads started showing up and getting ugly. Then it was time to quit. Besides, your father graduated and wanted to move back to LA."

"I can't believe you met in a punk club." Grady returned the ice cream to the freezer.

"Yeah," Rowan continued when he returned. "Earl was the most unlikely guy I'd ever seen at one of our gigs. That's why I let him buy me a drink."

Grady changed the channel and paused at a speech by Dick Cheney, who wore his customary blue suit, red tie, and American-flag lapel pin. His aquiline nose, fleshy face, and halo of silver hair gave him an air of thoughtfulness. Cheney spoke with his usual gravitas stating his belief that Saddam Hussein would soon have nuclear weapons.

"Jesus!" Grady turned off the TV. "Guess I'll go to bed."

"Good night."

He didn't sleep. The image of the prostitute with the glasses flickered in Grady's mind. He knew he should exile her from his thoughts but he could almost feel the warm, damp touch of her. Around 3:00 AM he decided he had to act.

The next morning Grady put on his pants and pulled a dirty polo shirt over his head. It seemed like he'd just washed everything but nothing was clean. After breakfast he excused himself from the day's sightseeing by saying he was getting together with Willem from the aikido dojo instead. His parents did not protest. In fact, from the way their bodies relaxed Grady had the sneaking suspicion that they were relieved. He set out full of anticipation. Even his sore wrist felt better.

He made it to the Red Light District a little after 11:00 AM. Several prostitutes were already working the windows but there were fewer johns than at night. A blonde tapped the glass but Grady kept walking. He knew who he wanted if only he could find her. It took forty-five minutes but Grady finally located the coffee shop and scouted the nearby windows but his favorite woman was not there.

Grady entered the coffee shop. He still had some dope left so he ordered a coffee, sat down, and rolled another joint. Although the high wasn't as intense as the previous night's, he did spend over a few hours nodding to the reggae blaring from the sound system.

Eventually, the torpor cleared from his mind. Grady rotated his head to loosen the muscles in his neck and stepped outside. The curtain in his favorite girl's window was drawn. She was in! Grady returned to the coffee shop, dashed to the men's room, emptied his bladder into a urinal with mothballs by the drain, and went back outside in time to see the curtains open and the john step into the street. The man stood for a minute looking for a sign to get his bearings. Grady recognized the thinning blonde hair and peanut-shaped head. It was his father!

Grady ducked inside so his father wouldn't see him. What the hell was his dad doing there? Well, Grady knew what his father had been doing but where was Rowan and more importantly what should Grady do now? Chip off the old block? Like father like son? Should he screw the same woman his father had so they could compare notes? The thought turned his stomach.

Grady bought some more dope, smoked himself numb, and sat around for a few hours. Still stoned, he left the coffee shop and set off down the street. Two white-shirted policemen were talking to the driver of a Volkswagen. They ignored Grady staggering past. Working girls tapped their windows but he took no notice. He heard a bell and a bicycle whizzed by missing him by millimeters. Coming to the Red Light District had been a mistake. He saw that now. No matter how pretty the girl, it would always be about the money, not about him. He found that more than a little sad.

Grady ended up on a bench next to a canal. Nearby a houseboat with a black hull and white cabin was tied up. From the vessel's blunt shape Grady almost expected Noah and two of every creature to be onboard. He didn't see a giraffe head sticking through the roof so he supposed there was little chance of flood. An old guy with a gray beard and no mustache came up on deck. He said something in Dutch.

"I'm sorry," Grady replied.

A speedboat motored by with music playing from its stereo.

"I said it's a beautiful day."

And it was. The sky was clear and the sun was warm on Grady's skin.

"You live on that thing?" Grady asked.

"For over twenty years."

"No shit! What's it like?"

"Come on board. I'll show you."

Grady crossed the gangway and followed the man down into the hold. The interior was spacious and had a hardwood deck. Grady's host retrieved two bottles on Heineken from the refrigerator, removed the caps, and handed Grady one.

"*Proost.*" He touched his bottle's neck to Grady's and took a drink.

"So where's the motor?" Grady asked.

"There isn't one. It's just for living." The man climbed back out on deck and Grady followed. "The big hotels have offered me a half million euros for my mooring space but I wouldn't live anywhere else."

"Why's that?" Grady leaned against the rail.

"Where else can you have a beer on a houseboat on a Saturday morning?"

"Doesn't it bother you living next to prostitutes and sex shops?"

"I don't bother them and they don't bother me."

Grady chatted with the old guy for an hour before continuing his wanders. It had been almost two weeks since he'd checked his e-mail so he made that a priority. Some squatters had opened an Internet café in an abandoned building. Dinosaur PCs with CRT monitors the size of brontosauruses filled the room. The staff didn't charge Grady to use the Jurassic equipment, though. He had to ask for help with the Linux operating system but once he got Firefox running, he was able to log into his account.

OBgrrl@yahoo.com
Dear Grady,
I haven't heard from you. Are you mad at me?
Marisol

Oh shit! Grady deleted some junk mail and scrolled to Marisol's next message.

OBgrrl@yahoo.com
Dear Grady,
I still haven't heard from you so I guess you're pretty pissed off. Don't you think I'm disappointed too? Believe me. I'd rather be with you in Europe, Asia, or Tierra del Fuego than anywhere else. If there were a way to make it happen, I'd do it. Instead I'm stuck selling stupid hotdogs at the stupid mall. Grady, it really breaks my heart that you don't see that.
Marisol

Grady clicked the reply button.

gsankyu@hotmail.com
Dear Marisol,
Sorry I didn't write earlier. We were on a cruise with these awful people and I guess your message just pushed me over the edge. Things are better in Amsterdam. Marijuana is legal here, too. My parents have been sneaking off a lot. I think they're toking up. Can you believe it?
Grady

He paused at the keyboard. Should he mention his dad's visit to the Red Light District? He needed to talk to somebody but Marisol might wonder what he'd been doing there. Grady clicked Send and his message winged off into cyberspace.

He bought a picnic lunch and spent the afternoon at the Oosterpark. They had a drumming circle and he danced with some wild girls in shorts and tie-dyed T-shirts. From the way their breasts bounced when they jumped, it was obvious they weren't wearing bras. Grady tried to talk to them afterwards. Both said they had to go so he wandered around the Central Station and found a cool, hemp jacket. With the exchange rate it cost over two hundred dollars but what better way to spend the money he'd saved by not paying for sex? Grady bought it and returned to the hotel. His parents weren't there, which was fine. He didn't want to look at his father.

No excuse could get Grady out of the Sunday poker game. He took his place at the kitchen table while Rowan counted out pennies, pence, and the euro equivalent.

"You father and I have been talking." Rowan looked to Earl and back to Grady. "You know, marijuana is legal here and we thought that if you want we could go to one of the coffee shops." She shuffled and dealt everyone two face down cards.

Grady liked his Jack and Queen of Hearts. He pushed a penny forward.

"It's only for here." Earl rapped the table. "Don't you dare try this anywhere else!"

"Of course, it's only if you want to." Rowan dealt the flop.

"I saw an ad for one." Grady took out his map and pointed. "It's on the Oudezidjs Achterburgwal in the Red Light District. Raise." Grady pushed four coins forward.

"Fold." Earl's face went white.

Rowan folded and Grady raked the coins into his stack. He bluffed Earl into folding a few hands later when he held only a Seven and a Two. Rowan called him.

"Okay." She nodded looking at Grady's trash hand after the showdown. "Okay." She stood from the table. "That's enough."

On his final night in Amsterdam, Grady visited the coffee shop in the Red Light District one last time but the novelty had worn off. He smoked the rest of his weed more out of nostalgia than desire. After an hour of listening to ska on the coffee shop's sound system, he walked through the crowd of anxious men but he felt little of their desperation. At the edge of the Red Light District a bottle blonde with wide cheekbones tapped her window to get Grady's attention. He turned and saw the blonde expose a penis from under his panties. A transvestite! Really? Grady shook his head and walked away.

CHAPTER 9

OBgrrl@yahoo.com
Dear Grady,
I survived my first week at U Dub. My dorm room's OK except for that bitch across the hall. I had to tell her to turn her music down at 2:00 AM twice already. Do you know how to sabotage a CD player? Don't even ask about the cafeteria food. It makes anorexia look good.

Seriously, my classes are OK. I pulled a 7:30 anatomy class but I can cope. Lisa, her boyfriend Dan, and I went to the Bumbershoot festival and saw some cool bands. She lives on my floor. They're from South Bend. As soon as the festival was over, it started to rain. They say it'll last until July. Oh well.

Hope you mom's OK.
Bye Puffins,
Marisol

Passports in hand Grady and Earl stood behind the yellow line waiting for the Estonian immigration official to call them. They'd just gotten off the ferry from Helsinki in Tallinn. Prague was flooded so they went north after Amsterdam. Traveling through Scandinavia, Grady had treated Earl as coldly as Norway's glaciers but he had kept his father's visit to the Dutch prostitute a secret. After a few days in Helsinki, Rowan had packed the two men off on this side trip. She'd said she wouldn't dream of letting them miss the well preserved medieval city with its narrow, winding streets she couldn't navigate with her sore knee. Grady suspected it was a ruse to allow him and his father to clear the air. Fine! If she wanted to put up with the cheating son of a bitch, it wasn't his problem.

The official motioned to them. Grady followed his father forward, crossing the yellow line into the Former Soviet Union. Images of intrigue from all those 1980s movies played in Grady's head – Sean Connery and Michelle Pfieffer in Moscow, Sean Connery and a runaway nuclear submarine under the Atlantic, and Clint Eastwood in a stolen Soviet jet. Grady's pulse quickened as he laid his passport on the gray-faced official's desk. Thunk went the stamp! That was all.

They found a taxi outside. The driver filled the closed interior with choking, blue cigarette smoke while tapping his fingers on the steering wheel to the tempo of the Europop on the radio. Cars slowed traffic from the ferry terminal to a standstill. Grady longed to roll down a window but feared he'd violate some national taboo.

Workers were digging up underground storage tanks with a miniature, orange backhoe by a gas station. Once they passed, traffic sped up. Grady saw the eight hundred-year-old walls and towers of the old city on the right but to his disappointment the driver took a left at the intersection and ventured into the wasteland left by Tallinn's former Soviet occupiers. Aside from a few convenience stores, the landscape looked like it had been devastated by blockbuster bombs. There were abandoned factories behind rusting fences, dreary apartment complexes with peeling wooden facades, and ruined industrial buildings with their walls reduced to rubble. One of the latter sported a blue awning and sign for a nightclub inside.

Unlike its surroundings the hotel was clean and modern, four stories across from a grassy park. Inside a bearded man in shorts and a dirty T-shirt was delivering a slurred tirade to the desk clerk. After repeated refusals from the desk clerk the man turned away and weaved toward the elevator. Even from the distance, Grady could smell the liquor fumes on the man's breath.

"Finnish people." The desk clerk shook his head and handed back Earl's passport. He was clean-shaven, neatly groomed, and resembled the immigration official in being nondescript, neither dark nor blonde, and neither heavy nor thin. He swiped Earl's credit card and gave him a room key.

Grady and his father climbed the stairs to their second-floor room. Grady tossed his bag on the twin bed closest to the window and turned on the TV. He switched from Estonian, Finnish, and Russian channels to the BBC. Secretary of Defense Rumsfeld was telling about a link between Iraq and Al Qaeda. Earl came out of the bathroom and sat on the bed to watch.

"You think there's going to be a war?" Grady asked.

"It's all saber rattling to scare Saddam into letting the weapons inspectors back it." Earl stood. "Feel like taking a walk to the old city? After sitting around with your mother I could use some exercise."

"All right." Grady grabbed his jacket.

On foot they got a better view of the abandoned factories than from the speeding taxi. Two sooty smokestacks still stood but all the windows and doors had been broken or removed. The ground was barren dirt except for a few spindly weeds hearty enough to grow in the poisoned soil. What paint there had been on the walls had worn to a few white patches on grimy brick.

"The Russians sure left this place a mess," Grady said.

"That's communism for you," Earl said. "There are problems with capitalism but at least it gives you an incentive to work."

The problems with capitalism soon became apparent in the sprawl of convenience stores and fast food outlets they found on the way to the city center. Earl changed some money at a bank.

"Look at this." He handed Grady a blue banknote. "The woman on the hundred, Lydia Koidula, is a poet."

Grady examined the portrait on the bill. "Sure beats using politicians."

"Finland and Estonia are founded on poetry."

"What do you mean?"

"The common peoples' language sets them apart from their conquerors. By celebrating it they affirm their identity." Earl thumbed through the guidebook. "Let's take a little detour."

The walked several blocks to a bronze statue of a Soviet soldier. The standing, bareheaded figure was executed in the crude, Stalinist style to celebrate the replacement of Nazi totalitarianism with the Soviet version. Someone had placed flowers in the crook of the soldier's bent arm and a bouquet at his feet.

"The locals hate this." Earl removed the camera from his fanny pack.

"Why don't they just tear it down?"

"Don't want to upset their powerful neighbor to the east, I imagine. Yeah, must be a hell of a thing living next to a sleeping bear and knowing it could wake at any moment." Earl pointed to a spot next to the statue. "Why don't you stand over there so I can get a picture?"

Grady moved over and rested his hand on the cold metal.

"You think we did the right thing leaving mom in Helsinki?" he asked.

"You can't expect her to put up with us twenty-four-seven. Even she needs a rest some time." Earl snapped the picture. "If I know your mother she's in a sauna with a good book and a cold beer right now."

"It's just that if something were to happen when we were gone…"

"She seems to be all right now, Grady. When she starts failing for good, we'll need to be there but for now let's just enjoy the day." Earl returned the camera to his fanny pack. "You about ready to get out of here?"

"All right."

They approached the old town from the west by crossing the train tracks at the station and paralleling the stone wall until they reached a medieval gate. A cylindrical guard tower with a red tile roof and narrow archers' windows protected it.

"Must have been hell trying to attack something like this armed with only a sword," Earl said. "Of course, now you'd just blow it up with cannons."

They passed through the arched gateway and strolled up a cobblestone street, surrounded by tall stone walls. They followed the signs to the town square with its whitewashed shops that dated back hundreds of years. Several had been turned into restaurants and diners sat on chairs set out in the square.

"Your grandmother used to tell me about this place." Earl pointed his camera at the stone Town Hall and zoomed out to fit the tower into the picture.

"Grandma Anna?"

"She was just a little girl when her family left." Earl snapped the photo and pointed to the tourists lined up by the Town Hall. "She never talked about why. I imagine my mother had to endure a lot of hardship she never told me about. Want to climb to the top?"

"All right."

Earl paid the entrance fee and after a brief wait led the way up the narrow, spiral staircase that wound like a screw's thread to the top of the six hundred-year-old tower. Having taken up the rear, Grady got an eye-level view of his father's butt. It reminded him of driving behind an SUV or being a child and having his view of a parade blocked by adults in front. When they got to the top, Earl was panting as if he'd climbed Everest carrying a hundred-pound pack. Grady vowed never to get that out of shape and moved to a window to admire the view.

A breeze blew through the open space and ruffled Grady's hair as he looked down at the sloped roof and the waiters carrying trays through the rows of tables set out by restaurants on the square. He raised his eyes to the panorama of towers, red roofs, and old churches. He and Earl traded places with other sightseers to view other portions of the old city before returning to street level.

"Did you ever want to join the army?" Grady asked.

"No. Vietnam had just ended when I was eighteen. Most of us wanted to stay as far away from the military as possible."

"'Cause, I don't know, maybe I could go ROTC to earn money for college."

Earl nodded but didn't comment.

At lunch Earl attempted to speak a few Estonian phrases. The waiter repulsed his efforts as if pouring boiling oil on an attacker from the castle wall above. Afterward Grady and his father wandered to the Lassi plats where the pink parliament building and the onion-domed Nevsky Cathedral eyed each other warily across the square. To satisfy their curiosity they entered the Russian Orthodox cathedral. At first Grady regretted dropping coins into the oppressors' donation box but the candles, icons, and white dove painted on the sky blue ceiling were beautiful

"Should we go see the Kiek in the Kök?" Earl asked when they stepped out of the dim church and into the sunshine.

"Sounds painful," Grady said.

"You're the karate student. You can handle it."

After they visited the unfortunately named cannon tower, Earl stuffed the guidebook into his fanny pack.

"Sometimes you spend so much time reading that you don't see the buildings," he said.

They wandered aimlessly through the old city and found a sign for the Brotherhood of Blackheads. Grady posed next to it and Earl took his picture. Although shamed by his previous attempt to speak the language, Earl tried his Estonian again at dinner with equally discouraging results. After sunset they caught a taxi. Earl had the driver stop in front of the abandoned factory that housed the nightclub. Dozens of people costumed like devils, frogs, and bears waited by the blue awning.

"If I were your age and missed a party like this, I'd regret it for the rest of my life." Earl handed Grady some money. "Why don't you go check it out?"

"You coming?" Grady reached for the door handle.

"You don't need your old man for this. Just don't wake me when you get back."

A picture of a poet gained Grady admission. He waded through a sea of writhing bodies and found a place to stand near a concrete wall. It didn't seem like his kind of scene but he supposed he should stay after all the fuss his father had made. It was a typical rave. More women than men danced to the recorded techno music that echoed off the hard surfaces. Many wore bikini tops to stay cool. Several dancers twirled light sticks. Grady's eyes eventually settled on a woman in a sleeveless blouse who made thrusting motions similar to karate punches with her arms. When she caught him looking, a satisfied smile formed on her lips as if his interest confirmed her belief that she was a trendsetter.

Grady was about to leave when he noticed a woman in a paper maché crocodile mask, her face protruding from between its jaws. The urge to know her overcame him but how could he do it? The music was too loud for conversation and he probably wouldn't understand her if they could speak. With no other options Grady made motions that resembled dancing and moved closer. That way he could almost believe he was dancing with her instead of by her. This went on for twenty minutes. Then the music stopped.

"Can I buy you a drink?" Grady asked.

"What?" She took off the mask and leaned closer. Her brown hair was soaked with sweat.

"Can I buy you a drink?"

"I have my own. Thank you." She took a water bottle from her pocket and drank. Grady was about to turn away when she said, "You look uncomfortable. Do you want to sit?"

They found a free table and Grady cleared it of napkins and plastic cups left by the previous occupants.

"What brings you here?" the woman asked.

"Just curious. I've never been to a nightclub in an abandoned factory."

"No, what brings you to Tallinn?"

"I'm traveling around the world."

"Ah, at such a young age. You must be wealthy."

"Well, my parents are with me."

Grady learned her name was Marina. She offered him some tiny, orange pills. Maybe he followed his father's advice or maybe he just wanted the girl to think he was cool but Grady took one. If he'd refused he'd look like a dork. They danced until the pill took effect making the sounds reverberate and lights diffract. Grady felt thirsty and dizzy.

Marina brought her lips close to his ear. "Want to see what is in the rest of the building?"

Grady nodded. She led him to the back of the nightclub, past a line of partiers waiting in a hallway to use the bathrooms, and through a fire door into the darkness. The drug made Grady see orange diamonds that pulsed to the beat of the music.

"What did they make here?" Grady shivered in the cold and damp and drew Marina close for warmth.

"Turrets for tanks." She led him deeper into the blackness.

"Where are we going?"

"It's a surprise." Marina tucked a finger into the waistband of his jeans. "Just a little bit farther."

Grady wondered if he was a fool for following. A lead pipe to the skull or knife to the kidneys could be hiding in the darkness to ambush him. And with the music blasting, no one would hear his shouts for help. It was probably innocent. Marina didn't seem like the kind of girl who would lead him into a trap. They walked on.

Instinct saved him. Whether it was the scuff of an approaching shoe or sensitivity to hostile ki, Grady sensed his opponents' approach. At the feel of two hands on his shoulders, Grady ducked under the thug's arms, grabbed one wrist in *sankyo*, and twisted eliciting a scream of pain from the first attacker.

Adrenaline cleared Grady's head. Still controlling the man's arm, he cut down bending the attacker forward but Grady stumbled on a brick and lost contact before he could take the man into a pin. It was just as well. Grady heard a whoosh and dodged some kind of club swung by a second man. It missed his head but glanced off Grady's shoulder. Grady kicked blindly in the direction of the second man, made contact with a leg, and heard the man curse.

By this time the first attacker had gotten back to his feet and grasped Grady from behind in a bear hug. Grady struggled back and forth to break the grip. His feet slipped against the wet concrete floor in an effort to keep from being pushed forward. It was no use. Time for a change in tactics. Grady went with the man's momentum and threw himself forward into a roll that took to thug to the ground and allowed Grady to break free.

Grady didn't wait around. While Marina shouted and the thugs swore, he scuttled into the darkness and hid behind a support beam. Clutching the cold metal he tried to slow his breathing so they wouldn't hear him. His shoulder throbbed. Eventually his eyes adjusted to the dark and he made out the shapes of the men searching for him. They never got close. After a half-hearted effort, they opened the nightclub door, creating a rectangle of light, and left. Grady shook from the aftereffects of combat. He'd been lucky. It hadn't been as pretty as aikido class but he'd survived. He pissed in the dark and waited an hour to make sure his attackers were gone. Then he exited through the nightclub and made his way back to the hotel. He had a hell of a story to tell but his parents would never hear it.

OBgrrl@yahoo.com
Dear Grady,

Help! Dan's been hanging around ever since Lisa broke up with him. I feel sorry for the guy but he's really getting on my nerves. I've got to find him a girlfriend so I can go back to studying. I got a B on my first anatomy test. That just won't do.

How was Copenhagen? Where are you now?
Hope your mom is OK.
Bye Puffins,
Marisol

CHAPTER 10

Dr. Chen clipped Rowan's x-ray to the light box and flipped the switch.

"The cancer has spread to your wife's leg." He pointed to the bulge on the long length of femur. Though Hong Kong Chinese, Dr. Chen spoke with an upper class British accent. "At this stage I would not recommend surgery. We can control local breakouts with radiation. Chemotherapy is an option but it's less effective the second time around. Of course, the choice is yours."

Grady thought it odd that the treatment choice would be Earl's and not his mother's but this was Asia after all. After a nervous week in Istanbul they'd traveled to Hong Kong because it was too early for Australia and fall was the best season to visit the southern Chinese city. By now most tourists had returned to their boring lives and the normally hot, humid weather was cool and pleasant. Rowan's sore knee had prevented her from enjoying herself, however. At Earl's insistence, she'd seen the doctor, which was why he and Grady were in the office while she sat in the waiting room.

"What would you do if it were your wife?" Earl asked.

Rowan was reading a copy of *People* when they returned to the waiting room.

"The doctor wants to treat your leg with radiation." Earl sat beside her and took her hand. "He says we caught it early and if the cancer shows up somewhere else, the radiation can knock that out too."

Rowan nodded as if she'd expected the news. "How long?" she asked.

"The treatment will take a few weeks. Then we'll be free to go."

They took a red-and-white Toyota taxi back to their lodging in Tsim Sha Tsui. In his haste to save money, Earl had booked a week's stay sight unseen at the Chungking Mansions, a sprawling complex of clothing shops, cheap eateries, and low-rent guesthouses on Nathan Road in Kowloon. Two elevators, the size of phone booths, served Block H. Unfortunately for the Evans there was always a line to use them. Grady would have preferred climbing to his destination despite the trash in the stairwell but due to his mother's bad leg he had to wait with the others. Eventually an elevator came and they rode it to the fourth floor.

Earl unlocked the Happy Family Guesthouse's outer steel door and ushered Rowan and Grady through the barricade and into the common area. A Chinese man in a sleeveless T-shirt waved from behind the front desk.

As he had the previous day, Grady retreated to his room. The bed took up most of the space leaving only a small area for his suitcase. Before stepping into the bathroom he stripped off his clothes, leaving his pants on the bed and stuffing the T-shirt and underwear into the laundry bag. The shower wasn't much, only a nozzle attached to the sink and a drain on the bathroom floor but at least it was private. Grady lowered the toilet seat, started the stream of lukewarm water, and wet himself under the hand-held nozzle. Using the flimsy sliver of soap, he scrubbed his skin clean of the hospital. Then with a tattered towel around his waist he stepped out of the bathroom and stood by the grimy window to look down on the trash strewn on the neighboring courtyard. What was life like in the dreary high rises that surrounded him? He didn't care to think about it. Instead he turned on the TV.

Even the most monotonous routine provides some comfort. Those who are frightened are especially likely to make it their refuge. The Evans fell into a routine that revolved around Rowan's treatment. Even though Rowan's therapy wasn't until 10:00, they woke at 6:30 to allow plenty of time to wait for the elevator and find a taxi to take them to the hospital. Grady and Earl would eat a quick breakfast of leftovers from the previous night's dinner, soymilk, fruit, and sometimes Chinese pastries in the common area before leaving.

Most days they arrived at the hospital early and had to sit in the waiting room. They were the only Caucasians. All other patients were Chinese. One middle-aged woman had a flap of smooth skin sewn over what had been the right side of her face. Grady did his best not to stare. Eventually, the Filipina therapist, a woman with a round face and bad complexion, would call Rowan's name and take her back to the linacs. Rowan would return ten minutes later with another square having been marked on her treatment chart and the Evans would retrace their steps back to the Chungking Mansions.

Rowan never wanted to stop for lunch after her treatment and once back in her room the elevator situation discouraged her from going out again. She never tasted the heavenly dumplings served from bamboo steamers in a dim sum restaurant or drank the tiny cups of powerful oolong tea with a Chiu Chow meal. She depended instead on the takeout food Grady brought back from the eateries nearby.

These errands were his only escape from the tiny room where he waited for requests from his parents and watched Japanese cartoons dubbed into Cantonese as well as the Senate debate on granting President Bush war powers. On these outings he would flee the Indian and African immigrants, swirling in the Chunking Mansions' ground floor shops, and escape onto Nathan Road. The air smelled of five-spice powder, fried food, and diesel fumes. Occasionally, Grady caught a whiff of sewage. Camera shops and jewelry stores lined the street and tailors called out, "Sir! Sir! A suit for only one hundred dollars! Please come inside." Someone else's foot seemed to occupy the space on the sidewalk every time Grady tried to take a step.

The days drifted by, one like the next. The news showed a Bali nightclub bombing. Weeks later, Chechen rebels took hostages in a Moscow theater. None of this affected him as neither spot was on their itinerary. Lulled by the days' sameness, Grady could almost imagine his mother would be with them for years to come. He liked to walk at night best when Chinese couples strolled arm-in-arm browsing in shop windows. Neon lights seduced him into side streets. He wandered the alleyways near Hanoi Road and ate in open-air cafés to feel part of the surge of humanity. Sometimes he went to Temple Street where fortunetellers read their customers' faces and performers sang Chinese opera outside with a full orchestra. His parents weren't adventurous about what they ate so he picked up safe dishes like General Tso's chicken or beef with broccoli and carried them back in Styrofoam containers.

One night Rowan answered the door.

"Earl stepped out for some air." She stood aside to let Grady enter.

Styrofoam containers that had held previous meals overflowed the trash can and the air was thick with the smell of uneaten food. Grady made his way between the violet travel bags and set the plastic bag on the nightstand. Rowan sat on the bed next to an open copy of *Super System*, the bible of poker players. Grady stood shifting his weight from one foot to the other.

"Sorry I won't make it to Japan with you. I was looking forward to having you explain about the samurai and all." Rowan peeked into the bag of food but left it untouched. "I want you to go. I want you to see everything you can – the castles, the swords, the aikido masters. Maybe you can even find yourself a Japanese girlfriend."

"Mom, of course, you're going to make it to Japan." Grady sat on the corner of the bed. "And when you do, it's going to be great! You know why? Because of Zen! In Zen even the most insignificant act is an offering to Buddha. That's why Japanese pay such phenomenal attention to detail, from a master gardener sprinkling a few fallen leaves on a newly swept path to a CEO's focus on the long term instead of a quick buck.

"My sensei told me all the best places to go. They have Masamuni swords in the Tokyo National Museum and we can hear bands playing out on the street in Harajuku on Sundays. We'll go inside the big Buddha at Kamakura and then head up to Nikko for Tokugawa Ieyasu's tomb. And the food! Sushi caught hours before reaching your table! We can stay at a traditional inn, head down to Kyoto and Nara to the temples, and ride the bullet train that goes two hundred miles per hour but is so smooth it feels like you're standing still. The baths too! I hear Himeji castle is awesome!"

A key turned in the lock and Earl entered.

"What's going on?" he asked.

"Grady was telling me about Japan."

"Is that so?" Earl made a beeline for the food and looked in the bag. "Damn! They never give us enough napkins."

"Well." Grady stood. "Guess I'll be going."

"Stay for dinner if you want," Earl said between mouthfuls of chicken.

"Nah, I already ate." Grady maneuvered between the suitcases to get to the door. "See you in the morning."

The next day Rowan broke the tedium during a taxi ride to the hospital. "I want to go to Macau. I want to play some real poker players just once before I die."

"You finish your treatment next week," Earl said. "Why don't we go then?"

"Why not today?" Rowan said.

At the hospital the Filipina therapist gathered them in a tiny room and said, "If you stop your treatment, the cancer will come back."

"It's only for a few days," Rowan replied.

"Have to add more treatment at the end." The therapist took a pen from the pocket of her white lab coat and pointed to the chart. "More complications."

Rowan remained adamant. Grady wondered if the therapist was truly concerned for his mother's welfare or only miffed at having to rework the treatment schedule.

After leaving the hospital and gathering their bags, they had only a short wait at the ferry terminal before boarding the jetfoil. Within minutes the powerful engines roared and the boat skimmed across the Pearl River Delta. Spray punctuated the windows with water droplets. To the left the green-and-white Star Ferry transported passengers between Kowloon and Hong Kong Island where angular skyscrapers sprouted like quartz crystals from the rolling green landscape. The jetfoil left the city behind and dodged rusty freighters flying Chinese flags in the waters separating Hong Kong's other islands. Within an hour the boat arrived at the dock in Macau where once again the Evans stood behind a yellow line awaiting entry into a new country. What would this one bring? Grady's mother was weakening. Would this be the land of orphans?

After clearing immigration they took a taxi to the Hotel Lisboa, a pink, cylindrical building on the water. Its spacious rooms were a relief after being cooped up in the Hong Kong guesthouse. And since the casino was across the courtyard, Rowan would have only a short walk to her destination.

She changed into black slacks, a deep blue blouse, and a pearl necklace that lay against the aging skin of her neck. Carrying a tiny purse and the aluminum cane from the hospital, she walked with Grady and Earl to the casino's cashier where she began signing traveler's checks. The cashier asked to see her passport. Rowan laid the rumpled document on the counter and kept signing. The cashier returned this and exchanged the traveler's checks for a tray of poker chips.

"Would you carry these for me, please?" Rowan handed Grady the tray.

She led them through rooms full of eager suckers feeding banks of slot machines, roulette wheels, and blackjack tables. Some would have found the atmosphere electric but to Grady it was a bore. He pitied the gamblers jabbering in Cantonese while wasting money on the futile hope of a big win. Rowan didn't see it that way. Maybe gambling came naturally when you played the odds for your very life.

A chest-high partition separated the poker room from the rest of the casino. Inside the hush of concentration replaced the din of slot machines. Here was a sober crowd intent on winning. The host identified the no-limit table and Rowan paused to study the players. The dealer was a plain, Chinese woman in black slacks and white blouse. Once she laid cards on the green felt, the betting started. Having already wagered their chips, the blinds, a young woman in a black gown and a young man in a silk sports jacket and black open-collared shirt, did nothing. A farmer with a tanned face and graying flattop haircut pushed forward his chips as did the dragon lady seated to his left. She sported a red cheongsam and wore her hair in a beehive. The pale, pancake makeup did little to disguise her age. Other players made their bets. A baby-faced man, the only non-Asian at the table, made a joke in fluent Cantonese, and a middle-aged man in a gray suit and white baseball hat peered at the others through bifocals before throwing in his cards. Rowan watched them play several hands before whispering, "I can beat these guys."

"Deal me in." Rowan hooked her cane on the edge of the table and sat.

"You need anything else, mom?" Grady set the chips down beside her.

"No thanks. Why don't you check back with me in an hour or so?" She lit a cigarette and examined the two cards she was dealt.

"What do you want to do now?" Grady asked his father.

"Guess I'll play a few slots," Earl said.

Grady followed his father out of the poker room and abandoned him when he sat down with the rest of the automatons to play. The sounds, flashing lights, and garish decorations seemed to siphon attentiveness out of Grady's skull. How could anyone concentrate in such an atmosphere? Maybe that was the idea. Still, it was good training for a martial artist. If Grady could keep his mental focus here, he'd be able to do the same anywhere. What was it about people that made them want to risk their children's education on a toss of the cards? Grady didn't know but judging from the island's casino construction boom, the urge must be widespread. He took a seat at an empty slot machine, inserted a coin, and pushed the glowing button. The three dials spun and came to rest on a seven, a dog, and a lemon. Grady was out one Hong Kong dollar. What fun!

When he stood to leave, the hunchbacked granny, feeding coins from a plastic bag into the machine next to his, looked at him and shook her head. Maybe his study of martial arts could be a bridge to help understand his mother's obsession with gambling. If seen as a form of combat, poker's emphasis on deception and the ability to read one's opponents had a lot in common with aikido. Of course, card games depended on chance while the true martial artist made his own luck through hard training. Maybe that's why the Chinese were so fond of gambling. Their lives were subject to natural disasters and arbitrary government decrees unlike in America where a man can make his own destiny. A gambler blew on the pair of dice cupped in his hands before shaking them at a blackjack table. Poor bastard!

Grady left the casino and entered a glitzy shopping mall, where consumer culture had a uniquely Asian flavor with vases and ceramic horses in shop windows. He ordered a bowl of fried noodles in a fast food shop. Unlike Grady the Chinese diners held bowls to their faces, shoveled food into their mouths with chopsticks, and sucked it in with slurping noises.

Grady returned an hour later to find the same players at his mother's table. Rowan had a cigarette burning in the ashtray and her pile of chips seemed a bit larger. Most players were smoking. The dragon lady held her cigarette an inch from her mouth as if afraid someone would steal it. The farmer chewed a sandwich with his mouth open, treating everyone to a view of saliva and masticated bread. The baseball hat man quietly pushed his bet forward.

"You need anything, mom?"

"Would you get me a bottled water?" Rowan withdrew some money from her purse and handed it to Grady.

He returned a few minutes later with her drink. Bored with the mall Grady went outside and walked inland on the Avenida de Almeida Riviero. A slim woman took his arm.

"Hey, you want to party?" Her large, brown eyes seemed drugged with hormones and her skin had the youthful blush of a ripe peach. No doubt the breasts under her loose blouse would be as soft.

Grady shook his head and walked to the square across from the senate. The buildings were painted in warm pastels as if they'd been frosted with butter cream and their trim decorated with a pastry bag. Inspired by the scenery he felt the urge for dessert. The bakery he found was run by Chinese and the moon cake, with its heavy lotus-seed filling and egg yolk center, wasn't exactly what he'd had in mind. He washed it down with a pot of jasmine tea before returning to the casino.

Rowan's stack of chips had shrunk by a third. From the set of her mouth Grady could tell the atmosphere at the table had turned serious as if she were playing with Yama King of the Dead for stakes a lot higher than the chips on the table. Four cards lay on the green felt: a Four of Clubs, Three of Hearts, Ten of Hearts, and Jack of Hearts. The man in the hat pushed forward a hundred dollars in chips. Rowan matched him and the farmer folded. The dealer laid a Ten of Diamonds on the table. Rowan smiled and turned over two hearts. The hat turned over a Ten and a Jack giving him a full house that beat Rowan's flush. The smile left her face as the dealer raked the chips toward the man in the hat.

"Grady," Rowan said. "Go get your father."

Grady didn't find his father near any of the gaming tables so he searched for the exit but kept making false turns that returned him to the slots. He hated them. To him the environment was as toxic as a malaria outbreak at the Hanford nuclear reservation. Electric sounds and flashing lights from the slot machines seemed timed to induce seizures and cigarette smoke scratched his throat like a rabid, gray cat. Eventually he made his way back to the hotel but Earl wasn't in his room. Grady returned to the casino and ran into Earl coming out of a men's room.

"Mom wants to see you." Grady escorted his father to the poker table.

"What took you so long?" Rowan asked.

She conferred with Earl in tense whispers. From his vantage point Grady heard only the phrases, "waste of money." and, "Don't ruin my chances." After several minutes Earl walked away and brought back another stack of chips.

"Good luck." He set them down and watched with Grady as Rowan lost a bluffing contest with the farmer.

"Grady." Rowan took some money from her purse. "Would you

get me a coffee, black?" She lit another cigarette and turned her attention back to the cards.

It had been hours since his mother had eaten so Grady got her a sandwich too. After delivering these he walked outside again. It was dark but Grady wasn't hungry. When he returned to the poker table, the sandwich he'd set by Rowan remained uneaten. She sat askew favoring her sore hip and her pile of chips had shrunk as if they'd been transformed into the cigarette butts crowding her ashtray. The game went on. Rowan struggled against the tide of loss like a rescue worker piling sandbags against a flood. The inexorable play of chance wore her down until she had only a hundred dollars of chips left.

"Get your father," she said to Grady.

This time Grady found Earl at the casino buffet. Together they returned to the table.

"You need to take a rest, Rowan."

"Earl, I know I can win this if you can just spot me another five hundred dollars."

"You've lost over two thousand. It's time to quit."

"This is my last chance to hit it big. Are you going to take that away from me?"

Earl remained silent.

"All I'm asking is for you to believe in me," Rowan said.

"Fine," Earl sighed.

He bought her more chips. Rowan lost these too. At 1:30 in the morning Earl refused her plea for more. Just like her piles of chips Rowan seemed to have diminished at the poker table. She fumbled with her cane in an attempt to stand. Grady rushed forward and helped her to her feet. She let him take her weight and raised herself to full height for the slow walk out of the casino. For all her dignity she might have been an elderly monarch reviewing her troops for the last time.

The sound of a baby wailing woke Grady that night. He pulled the covers over his head. Why couldn't that woman keep her kid quiet? The volume decreased as if the child had grown exhausted but kept crying out of stubbornness. Grady went back to sleep. He dreamed of the old golden retriever struggling to rise on stick-like legs from the doggy bed and wagging her tail at Earl who held the leash. Grady wasn't yet four but he sensed that somehow the dog wasn't coming back. With big tears in his eyes he ran toward her to stop the injustice.

"Hey." Rowan took his hand and swept him into her arms. "It's all right. Dad's going to take her to live on a beautiful farm where there are trees, and horses, and a lake, and lots of other dogs to play with." She took him into the kitchen and let him eat a lump of cookie dough while she cut the rest into cylinders and placed them on a baking sheet.

Grady woke and looked at the clock. It was 4:00 AM. The screams weren't from a baby. They were coming from his parents' room. He struggled into his clothes, went into the hall, and knocked on their door. Earl answered.

"Go back to sleep, Grady. The hotel summoned a doctor. I'll take care of this." Earl closed the door.

Grady stood in the hall in his bare feet.

OBgrrl@yahoo.com
Dear Grady,

Ever hear of Theatre Sports? It's an improvisation contest where teams get points for making the audience laugh. I liked it so much that I took a few workshops. You'll never believe it but I'm now on a team called the Wallingford Wailers. I didn't want to tell you I tried out before, in case I didn't make it. Anyway, my first competition will be this Friday. Dan's so jealous. Wish you could be there.

Bye Puffins,
Marisol

CHAPTER 11

The driver with mahogany-colored skin loaded passengers' bags into the tiny trailer and offered his arm to help Rowan into the van. As Grady took a seat next to his mother, he wondered how the man could maneuver the van and trailer through busy city traffic. Earl and the others climbed on board. Grady examined the passengers. He would have talked to the woman with the pale eyebrows and dyed, black hair but her boyfriend with the pierced lip probably wouldn't appreciate it. Speaking with an accent that was pure Australian the driver radioed to announce he was leaving the airport and heading toward downtown Sydney.

"They have a harbor cruise and a tour of the Opera House." Earl set pamphlets on Rowan's lap. "Sound like fun?"

Rowan shook her head. Ever since the night in Macau her lucidity came and went due to the pain medication.

"Or we could send Grady on the bridge climb," Earl said.

"You're going with me." Grady mock punched his father in the arm. "We can't let dad chicken out. Can we, mom?"

Rowan didn't answer. The driver got off the freeway, made several seemingly impossible turns, and stopped in front of a motel located between and adult book store and a Chinese cafeteria.

"Player's Motel, Kings Cross." He got out and removed the pierced couple's bags from the trailer before climbing back in and merging into traffic.

"Did you ever see that movie *Walkabout?*" Rowan asked.

"No, mom. What's it about?"

"These children get abandoned in the Australian outback and an Aborigine rescues them. There's a cute scene where the girl wakes up with a wombat looking over her shoulder. I'd sure love to see one."

"A girl or a wombat?" Grady asked.

"You see lots of wombats dead on the highway," the driver said. "Of course, you might be able to see one at the Taronga Zoo. Get there early in the morning or late in the evening, though. They sleep during the day."

Their hotel was located in a high rise about a dozen blocks from the harbor. After helping Earl get Rowan situated, Grady found his room, stripped, and stepped into the shower. When he closed the glass door, he found moths the size of his finger buzzing near the ceiling. It was creepy standing naked and vulnerable close to such alien things but Grady showered without being strafed. Afterwards he dried off, turned on the fan to clear the humidity, and stepped into the room with the towel wrapped around his waist.

Grady found more of the moths by the window when he opened the curtains. All were dark gray and sported wings that looked like fur-lined capes. There was something eerie about the way they perched on the wall and curtain rod as if unconcerned by his presence. He'd read somewhere that natives believed their dead returned as moths but didn't recall which natives. If he complained to the front desk, they'd spray the room full of poison. He didn't want that so he decided the moths probably belonged here more than he did. While he dressed, Grady watched the news on TV. The Republicans had taken the Senate. He felt guilty about missing the election but how could he have voted from overseas and would his vote have changed the outcome? Grady went to his parents' room to check about dinner.

"I just gave your mother her pain meds so she'll be out for a while." Earl's eyelids seemed heavy as if he'd been napping. "Why don't you get something to eat? I'll stay and watch her."

"Okay," Grady said. "I'll check back in an hour."

Grady took the elevator to the lobby, passed through revolving door onto the crowded sidewalk, and nearly got mowed over by rush-hour pedestrians who moved with a get-out-of-my-way determination that would do New Yorkers proud. He found a cheap Indonesian restaurant and ordered a fried rice dish he'd once heard referred to as, "nasty gory." The mostly Asian crowd took up the downstairs tables so he had to go to the second floor to find one that was free. A waitress brought him his order, which he smothered in hot sauce for a mouth-burning, nose-running feast. Grady then quenched the fire with jasmine tea before returning to his parents' room.

"She's asleep right now. Do you mind sitting with her while I get some dinner?" Earl retrieved the room key from the counter and left.

With eyes closed and breathing loud and labored, Rowan lay under the blanket on one of the twin beds. The sun had gone down, and lights from the office buildings made a spectacular view from the picture window. As in Grady's room the big moths opened and closed their wings near the glass. Grady shut the curtains and sat in the cone of light from a reading lamp paging through a tourist magazine he'd found on the table.

"Earl," Rowan whispered. "Earl, are you there?"

"It's Grady, mom."

"Would you get me a glass of water, sweetheart?"

Grady got a glass of water from the bathroom and set it on the table beside Rowan's bed. She made no effort to drink.

"Earl," Rowan whispered. "Your mother forgives you."

"Anna?" Grady spoke the name of his grandmother who'd died almost ten years ago.

"Yes. Anna knows you did the best you could." Rowan grew silent.

Grady read about the Harbour Bridge climb until Earl returned.

"She was saying something about grandma Anna." Grady said.

"It's the drugs." Earl set a white, carryout bag on the counter. "They knock her out for the first few hours. Soon we'll need to think about putting her in a hospital."

Grady returned to his room.

Rowan was better the next morning. Though weak she appeared rested and alert at the breakfast buffet.

"Are you up for a visit to the zoo today, mom?" Grady opened a yellow packet of Vegemite and spread the tarry substance on his toast.

"Oh, not today, honey. I want to rest a bit and catch up on my reading." Rowan ate a few bites of cereal and set the spoon down.

"Don't you want to see the wombats?" Grady bit into his toast and nearly gagged on a taste nothing could have prepared him for.

"Why don't you go and take some pictures with your father's camera? You can show me when you get back." Rowan winced. Her body relaxed when the pain passed.

"Are you okay, mom?"

She squeezed her eyelids closed and grimaced.

"Rowan, do you want to go to the hospital?" Earl touched her forearm.

"No more hospitals."

"How about a hospice?" he asked.

"Just let me rest a bit. I'll be fine in a few days."

"Let's go upstairs, Rowan." Earl helped her to her feet. "We'll get your pills." He removed the camera, a spare room key, and a few Australian banknotes from his fanny pack and put them on the table for Grady. "Get some pictures of the animals for your mother. She'd love to see them."

As Earl escorted Rowan to the elevators, the other diners turned their attention back to their meals. Grady finished his breakfast except for the Vegemite-smeared toast and walked toward the harbor.

The frantic, steamroller pace of people in business dress eased the closer he got to Sydney Cove. When he caught sight of the water, he snapped a photo of the Sydney Opera House, a white clamshell made tiny in the viewfinder by distance. Grady bought a zoo pass that included the ferry ride at the ticket office. Drawn by red, green, and beige mounds of ice cream in the window, shoppers lined up at the nearby gelato shop. Grady had a half hour before he had to leave so he bought a cup of cashew gelato and sat on a nearby bench. The sun was hot on his skin and the ice cream melted and dripped over his fingers. He fished a tube of sunscreen from his pocket and spread it on his face and arms. A white, goose-sized ibis with a black head probed the grass near Grady's feet with a bizarre beak that curled into a semicircle. There were ducks and seagulls nearby but these weren't as interesting as this strange creature. Grady found the ice cream too sweet for the early morning. After a few spoonfuls it left his mouth with a bitter aftertaste. He tossed the cup in the trash and made his way to the pier.

Two shirtless Aborigines set a hat on the pavement for donations and daubed each other's chests with white dots in preparation for some kind of street performance. Grady would have liked to see it but the ferry arrived before they began. He boarded and claimed a fiberglass chair on the top deck. Soon the engines roared and blew hot diesel fumes. The boat began to move. Though the wind chilled him, he braved the cold rather than join old people, mothers, and children with dripping Popsicles in the cabin. Bracing against the boat's rocking, he snapped pictures of the Harbour Bridge that looked like a giant child's erector set project gone horribly wrong. He pointed his father's camera at the giant face that marked the entrance to an amusement park on the north shore but it was too far away for a decent photo.

When the ferry arrived fifteen minutes later, a bus was waiting to drive the passengers uphill to the entrance. Some boarded. Others chose to pay extra to take the cable car. Grady did neither. Why coop himself up on such a gorgeous day? He took a picture of Sydney's skyline across the harbor and set off on the half-mile hike. The bus passed leaving him in a cloud of exhaust. Grady crossed to the right side of the road and began his hike from there. The vegetation was mostly scrub and eucalyptus. The sun was hot. He began to sweat and scratched under his money belt. Soon he grew short winded and paused to admire the boats plying the jewel-like harbor while he caught his breath.

He resumed his hike up the steep grade and made it to the entrance where an attendant stamped his ticket and gave him a map. Even though he'd developed a thirst, his first stop would be the wombats where he'd get his mother some great pictures. Grady folded the map and resigned himself to more walking, this time to the native animal display near the top of the hill.

Fortunately, he soon came across a market and bought a bottle of water. Oblivious to zebras and giraffes, Grady hurried up the path but stopped for a huge lizard sunning itself on the steps. A blue tongue extended from its open mouth.

"Jesus!" Grady said. "What the hell is that thing?"

"A blue-tongued lizard." A man in a khaki vest laughed and walked by.

Grady inched past half expecting the weird animal to lunge. Up ahead a five-year-old girl with loose blonde curls sang "The Kookaburra Song" while standing in front of a chain-link cage that held a spike-beaked bird with a crest that resembled Ronald Reagan's gelled pompadour. The nursery rhyme reminded Grady of a time when the world seemed a garden, not a jungle. He wanted to weep and could have listened all day but the father and daughter had already moved on.

When Grady arrived at the wombat enclosure it was empty except for a water dish and a hollow log. By craning his neck he could make out an animal's furry rear end inside the dark opening of the sun-bleached wood. Grady raised the camera and captured two megapixels of disappointment.

Nearby, visitors stood in line to enter a cage and have their pictures taken with a koala. Signs warned not to touch the cuddly critter that clung to with three-inch claws to a branch and nibbled eucalyptus leaves. Grady joined the queue. When it was his turn he handed Earl's camera to one of the female staff members.

"Does anybody ever try to pet him?"

"One did last week. Clyde opened a five centimeter gash in his forearm."

"Move a little closer." The other woman zoomed in and clicked the shutter. "I think I got a good one there. You mind if I try something a bit more artistic?"

Grady nodded and she took a half-dozen shots from various angles. He thanked her and went to look at the other animals. The red kangaroos seemed more interested in licking their forelegs than paying attention to the spectators. Grady saw wallabies, miniature kangaroos, and bettongs (even smaller kangaroos). Evidently nature loved the design of two strong hopping legs counterbalanced by a thick tail. He spent fifteen minutes looking through the glass at a pair of Tasmanian devils. The black, cat-sized animals walked with a roly-poly gate that belied jaws powerful enough to crush a leg bone. The zoo had an impressive reptile exhibit that included snaggle-toothed crocodiles with malevolent yellow eyes embedded in gray leathery skin.

Grady's favorite displays were of native birds, a rainbow of iridescent feathers. Wild birds, such as gray galahs, perched outside the cages to give moral support to their imprisoned brethren. A red-and-blue macaw regarded Grady, not unsympathetically, with eyes that resembled tiny licorice drops. Once again the world changed from jungle to garden as Grady realized that even when he felt alone, pairs of animal eyes were watching over him. The macaw squawked and flew away like a colorful kite with a broken tether.

Grady ate lunch at the Beastro and checked out the non-native animals. He liked sun bears and red pandas best. At around 2:30 he'd seen all he cared to see. He made one last stop at the wombat enclosure but they were still hiding. Grady took the cable car down to the harbor and caught the ferry back to the Circular Quai. Even though he had no decent shots of the wombats, Grady stopped by his parents' room to show his mother the photos he did get.

"Mom! Dad!" he called when no one answered his knock.

Grady inserted the key and opened the door. The afternoon light painted a beam in the dust motes floating by the window. Rowan lay propped up by two pillows in bed facing the male and female announcers silently moving their lips on TV. She'd combed her hair and put on lipstick.

"The wombat wouldn't come out but I got a few pictures of me with a koala." Grady scrolled through the camera's memory before suspecting something was wrong. "Why are you watching the TV without the sound?"

Rowan did not respond. Her vacant eyes stared without blinking. Only then did Grady realize his mother was dead. Her body was not creepy or frightening, just small and sad like his old Windows 98 computer after he'd replaced it. None of the moths were in the room. Grady turned off the television and sat by the bed. After a half hour he heard a key turn the lock. Earl entered and took in the sight of Rowan's body.

"Shit!" Earl dropped the bag of hamburgers, sank to his knees, and sobbed.

The coroner removed the body and after an hour of questioning the police seemed satisfied that Rowan's death was from natural causes. That night Grady and Earl ate dinner at the Indonesian place and strolled down to the Rocks, the quaint section near the harbor where Europeans first settled. There, tourists stood in line outside over-priced restaurants and music blared from the open doors of discos. They found a pub without much in the way of crowds and noise. Earl ordered two Victoria Bitters from a bartender with a beard down to his waist. Two women with bare navels hit balls on the pool table without much success.

"So, what are we going to do now?" Grady asked.

"Wait for them to release the body, I guess." Earl passed Grady a beer.

Grady watched one of the pool players bend over the table. Her shirt hiked up to reveal the white line of her panties and a butterfly tattoo between the dimples on the small of her back but he could not work up much interest. They finished their beers. Earl bought another round before he began talking.

"When you were a baby, your mother and I rented a house in Carlsbad. You were probably too young to remember Daisy, our golden retriever. She died when you were just three."

"I remember her," Grady said. "She was always digging up mom's flowers and she threatened to take her to the pound."

"That's right." Earl took a drink of his beer. "Anyway, I worked down in Sorrento Valley then and took the train every day. Regardless of when I got home, you, your mother, and Daisy were always waiting for me at the station. She said that stupid dog would pace by the door a few minutes before my train would get in.

"I remember standing at the station, the eucalyptus trees all around, my wife, son, and dog staring at me with adoring eyes, and the back of the train's red tail lights and blue-and-white warning stripes disappearing in the distance. And I recall thinking I was the luckiest man alive." Earl sniffled and wiped his eyes on his forearm. "Awe shit!" He finished his beer and set the glass on the bar.

"Too bad mom never got to see the wombat," Grady said.

"We haven't seen one either."

"Yeah, the ass end of one sleeping in a log at the zoo hardly counts."

"You about ready to get out of here?" Earl asked.

"All right."

Earl left a few bills on the bar and they went out into the warm, Sydney night. Absorbed in the historic atmosphere of the Rocks, strollers were oblivious to the two men's loss. As Grady passed a bouncer in a slouch hat and oilskin duster growled, "How're you going, mate?"

They walked to the waterfront and sat on a bench not far from the Harbour Bridge to admire the view. The Opera House seemed to glow like a ghostly set of sails in the nighttime illumination. They sat for a long time. Earl bent forward with his forearms on his thighs making figures in the dirt with his shoe.

"We don't have to continue." Earl straightened up. "I can get you on the next plane to Seattle. You'll be at U Dub in time to start the spring quarter."

Grady looked at his father. The man who'd made his teenage years a living hell seemed smaller as if Grady could crush him in his palm.

"I could go, I suppose," Grady said, "but then I'd never get to see the wombats. Mom would have wanted me to see them."

"Yeah, I guess she would have."

OBgrrl@yahoo.com

Dear Grady,

I hope this message finds you and your mom well. I didn't plan out it but things between Dan and me have gotten serious. I think it's best for you and me to break things off. Dan's a really great guy. If you saw how he makes me feel, you'd be glad for me.

I know you probably never want to speak to me again but I hope we can keep in touch. The time we spent together means a lot to me, Grady. You're a dear, sweet guy, and I'm sure a lot of girls would consider you a good catch. So get out there and go on lots of dates! Don't mope around. OK?

Marisol

Grady attacked the keys. Carried by the momentum of rage his words flew onto the screen.

gsankyu@hotmail.com
Dear Backstabbing Bitch,

No, in fact, my mom is not well. She's dead but I guess you wouldn't care about that being so busy fucking Dan! You sure picked a hell of a time to stab me in the back. Drop dead!

Grady

Grady stared at the cursor hovering over the send icon for thirty seconds. Then he changed his mind and clicked the x to cancel. The prompt asked whether he wanted to save the message for later. He pictured Marisol's face flushed with righteous rage when she refused the prom underwear check. He clicked discard.

The Internet café's clientele were mostly Grady's age. In one booth a young woman with Asian features huddled around the monitor with her fair-haired boyfriend. Grady studied them. The woman had a solid but pleasing figure. Despite this musculature she periodically erupted in girlish giggles. How sad, Grady thought, that a snowflake or speck of dust could turn their friendship into loathing. The woman laughed and wrestled control of the mouse from her boyfriend. Grady turned back to the monitor and composed a new message.

gsankyu@hotmail.com
Dear Marisol,
I'm sorry to hear you want to call it off but I suppose I'm not surprised. We're

in Australia and things couldn't be better. Mom's on a winning streak. She hit it big playing poker in Macau and walked out of the casino ten thousand dollars richer. Dad can't get her to spend any of it. She says she's saving it to bankroll my college fund. We're going to be traveling around the country by car so I may not be able to check my e-mail for several weeks.

Best wishes,
Grady

CHAPTER 12

It took the coroner a few days to release Rowan's body. While they waited, Grady went for walks in Moore Park and the Royal Botanical Gardens. The newspaper headlines talked about a UN resolution but he was too stunned to pay much attention. In the confusion someone, a nurse or social worker, handed him a pamphlet on grieving. Grady appreciated the sentiment but where was the help when he really needed it? Where was the help when he had to take his mother to the hospital? Where was the help when he had to listen to her puking? Where was the help when the insurance company refused to pay for her treatments? He crumpled the pamphlet and threw it in the trash. There seemed to be a lot of gay people in town.

The undertaker wanted several hundred dollars for a container for Rowan's ashes. Her gambling losses had left Earl a bit short so she would instead be completing the final leg of her round-the-world journey in an orange, Riva coffee can. With her death Grady and Earl could share the same motel room, thus cutting the cost of lodging almost in half.

They didn't need to inform Rowan's parents because they'd died when she was in her twenties. Earl delayed contacting other relatives and dealing with the insurance. Since hauling Rowan's purple suitcase around the world would be inconvenient, Grady and Earl would eventually remove a few keepsakes and donate the rest to a thrift store. They planned to tour Australia by rental car so they put Rowan's bag in the trunk and postponed the task.

Reasoning that his son, being the newer driver, would adapt more quickly to driving on the left, Earl suggested that Grady drive. So on a sunny spring day Grady and Earl stood in a car rental lot in Kings Cross while a metallic-blue Mitsubishi sedan pulled out of the garage. From where he stood Grady could see the brake lights burn red and the steam sputter from the exhaust pipe. Fear scoured his arteries with adrenaline as he stared at the immaculate finish. He would have felt a lot better if the car already had a few scratches to camouflage the dings he'd more than likely put on it during the trip.

A dark-skinned mechanic in spotless overalls got out from behind the wheel and opened the boot for Grady and Earl's luggage.

Together all three circled the vehicle in a search for damage. When none was found, the mechanic presented a clipboard and pen to Earl.

"Sign here, sir." He spoke with a British accent as if he was from the Caribbean.

Earl scribbled his signature and gave back the clipboard. The mechanic tore off the yellow copy, handed it over, and then abandoned Grady and Earl to the sea of wrong-sided drivers.

"You've got the helm." Earl retreated to the passenger seat like a nuclear engineer turning over responsibility for the reactor at Chernobyl.

Grady got behind the wheel and adjusted the seat and mirrors. Everything felt wrong. From his position on the right-hand side, the car stuck out way too far on his left. Grady took a deep breath and shifted into drive. He'd take it slow through city traffic. Once he got on the highway, everything would be fine. While waiting for a break in traffic, Grady flipped the turn signal. Windshield wipers swept across the glass in front of his face.

"Shit!" The bastards had put the turn signals on the other side. Grady stopped the wipers and flipped the lever on the right-hand side of the steering column.

Grady turned into the far-left lane and steered between the marks on the pavement. The sun shining through the glass had raised the car's interior to an uncomfortable temperature but Grady was too busy to attempt the air conditioning. So far so good. All he had to do was take it easy until he got out of the city. The light changed and he stopped at an intersection.

"This is really weird, dad."

"You're doing fine, Grady."

The light turned green. Unfortunately, a beige Toyota traveling perpendicular to Grady's path, had failed to clear the intersection. Grady waited for the driver to move until a horn sounded behind him. He inched forward, steered the awkward left side of the rental car around the Toyota's rear bumper, and hit the gas. The car moved forward, and Grady imagined the thrill of an entire continent of open road before him. Then he heard the sound of scraping metal.

"Well, I made it for one block at least." Grady pulled to the curb and shifted into park.

He and Earl got out and looked around the corner but the Toyota had already driven away.

"Don't worry about it." Earl clapped Grady on the shoulder. "I got the extra insurance."

They set off again. Earl spread a street map on his lap and called directions to Grady. After a nail-biting half hour, they merged onto a highway heading southwest. The plan was to head toward Canberra but rather than take the direct route they would drive along the coast and cut inland later. Grady aimed the car's hood between the white lines but felt that somehow he wasn't staying in his lane. Remembering his driving instructor's advice, he looked farther up the road and felt a bit better. Eventually he grew confident enough to pass a slow-moving camper van. Grady reached for the turn signal and activated the wipers again. He shook his head and used the lever on the opposite side of the steering column. Grady changed lanes, accelerated past the van, and returned to the left lane.

"Yeah!" Grady pumped his fist in the air.

He had little time to celebrate, however. Earl demanded that they stop for lunch at the next town. Grady's body tensed at the approach to Wollongong. With a thousand tiny needles of anxiety jabbing his neck, he turned on the blinker and exited into a maze of cross streets, stop signals, and even the dreaded traffic circles. He navigated these with competence if not mastery. The left-handed gods took pity on him by providing a space that didn't require parallel parking. They stopped at a café for sandwiches. Earl had one beer and then another. Grady drank a Pepsi. After an hour's stop they were back on the highway headed toward Nowra.

"There's supposed to be something interesting around here. I made a note about it but can't remember why." Earl put on his reading glasses and fumbled with the guidebook only to put it down in frustration when he couldn't find the right page.

Grady drove on while Earl fiddled with the radio eventually settling on a seventies rock station. The highway narrowed to two lanes and Grady got stuck behind another van. Suitcases and clothing packed the inside of the slow-moving vehicle and blocked the view from its rear window. Each time it was legal to pass, an oncoming car appeared in the other lane. After following the van for over ten kilometers Grady saw an opening, gunned it, and glided past. He glanced at the driver in a worn straw hat before returning to his lane. The open road ahead of him looked like freedom.

"Ever notice how most slow drivers ware hats?" Grady asked.

"There's a tourist information center." Earl pointed to a sign. "Pull over."

"And get trapped behind that asshole in the van again? No way!"

"Come on, Grady."

"I said I'm not going to do it. All right!"

They drove in silence. A few kilometers later Grady saw a sign for a park and swerved off the highway. Following the signs they came to a booth where a woman in khaki collected the ten Australian dollar entry fee. Soon the pavement ended. Their Mitsubishi bumped down the dirt road. Whenever a car passed going the other way, the cloud of dust it dragged obstructed Grady's view and layered the Mitsubishi with grit. After roughly fifteen minutes Grady pulled into a gravel parking lot and got out.

Grady retrieved some sunscreen from the back seat, smoothed the lotion on his face and arms, and circled the car. There was no way they'd slip that one past the rental return guy. The gouge he'd put on the fender had dug through the gray primer and exposed bare metal. Leaving his father behind, he walked a sandy trail that wound between trees and grasses and ended on a beach. The water was a clear aquamarine that partially covered vast stretches of porous, black rock near the shore. Grady knelt and picked up a handful of clean, white sand. It was soft between his fingers like brown sugar the instant you open the box.

"Grady!"

Grady turned and his father snapped a picture with the digital camera. He took off his shoes and socks, rolled up his pant legs, and waded in the water.

"Should have brought my swimming trunks," Grady said.

"They're in the car if you want to go back for them." Earl pointed the camera up and down the beach and snapped photos.

"I think I will." Grady went back and returned to change with a towel wrapped around his waist, thus shielding his modesty from the view of the couple fifty meters up the beach. "You watch my stuff?" Grady set his clothes down by where Earl sat.

"Okay."

"Let me know if you see any saltwater crocodiles or box jellyfish."

"Will do."

Grady waded into the warm water where unlike in Southern California he did not have to face the teeth-chattering decision to lower his belly into Pacific currents that might as well have been liquid helium. A whitecap rolled toward shore. Grady dived underneath and emerged spouting salt water on the other side. He tread water while bobbing with the waves for twenty minutes before heading to shore and sitting next to his father on the sand.

"You going in?" Grady asked.

"No, riding in a car for two hours with a wet crotch doesn't appeal to me," Earl said. "I've been thinking about you going into the army to pay for college. Don't do it or at least wait until this Iraq thing is sorted out."

"I'm surprised to hear you say that."

"If we go in, there'll be a lot of losses taking the cities."

"You think we will?"

Earl let out a breath. "There's no underestimating the stupidity of our leaders."

"But you're a defense contractor."

"Yeah." Earl ran a hand through his thinning hair. "There's not much else for a Ph.D. physicist to do. In graduate school, I didn't think it was going to be that way. It never occurred to me that someone with ten years of schooling couldn't find a decent job consistent with his pacifist morals or any morals for that matter. Academia got to be a burnout and all the corporations were closing their research centers."

"So, what did you do?"

"I wrote an SBIR grant for the most preposterous military project I could imagine," Earl said, "one that I was certain would never work, and the suckers bought it."

"What was it?"

"The phase-four missile defense system. You see, nuclear reactions vary depending on how the magnetic moments of the particles are aligned. So if you could use a magnetic field to turn the spins of neutrons and plutonium nuclei the wrong way, you might be able to turn a fission bomb into a fizzler."

"Sounds cool. Why wouldn't it work?"

"Because you could never make a magnetic field big enough to cover the volume you need. Well, maybe you could explode another nuclear bomb but that kind of defeats the purpose. Anyway, I've been milking the idea ever since. You know, instead of spending all that money on dorms, it might be better to buy you a house near the college." Earl tussled Grady's hair and got to his feet. "You ready to go?"

Grady drove for another hour before becoming too groggy to continue. They stopped at a motel in Batemans Bay, had dinner, and called it an early night. Earl's snoring kept Grady awake but after an hour he fell asleep. After breakfast they set off on the two-hour drive inland to Canberra, the nation's capital. Soon static interrupted the radio station that Earl had been listening to the previous day. He played with the tuner but found no suitable replacement.

"Why don't you let me drive?" Earl turned the radio off.

Grady pulled onto the shoulder and they changed places. Earl tripped the windshield wipers when attempting to signal before getting back on the road.

"It's on the other side."

"Right." Earl drove off.

"Move over a little." Grady pointed to the right. "You're driving on the shoulder."

Earl corrected the car's bearing but soon veered back to the left. Noting that his words had no effect, Grady kept his mouth shut but still flinched every time they passed a sign.

"I've been thinking about that casino in Macau," Earl said.

"What about it?"

"If only I hadn't cut your mother off, maybe she wouldn't have…"

"That's ridiculous, dad."

They approached a wallaby lying dead by the side of the road and the crow pecking its entrails flew away.

"I know. I just feel like I let her down somehow." Earl grew silent.

Grady turned on the radio to change the mood. He tuned into a station playing Aussie hip-hop.

"I don't understand how people can listen to that stuff," Earl said.

Grady switched the radio off.

"Sorry. I don't think I can do any more driving. You mind taking over?" Earl pulled over.

Grady drove the rest of the way. On the road to Canberra they counted two dead kangaroos, five wallabies, and numerous other creatures all mowed down by traffic.

"Those Aussies sure have it in for their wildlife," Grady said.

"Guess so."

Unlike in Sydney the traffic in Canberra was not overwhelming. Still, Grady was happy to leave the car in a parking lot once they'd found a motel. The proprietor gave them a key and a carton of milk for their tea. Grady and Earl had accumulated a week's worth of dirty laundry but Grady would let that wait until he saw the city.

"It's kind of a long walk into town but I'd just as soon not drive."

"I hear you." Earl peeled a hundred Australian dollars out of his billfold and gave these to Grady. "Why don't you go ahead? I'll stay here and maybe wash the dirty clothes."

"You sure?"

"Yeah."

By the time he'd walked four kilometers into town, Grady had worked up an appetite. The summer sun was strong and his face was no doubt burned. He wished he'd worn a hat. The Parliament House and fountain spraying water from Lake Burley Griffin looked inviting but the first order of business was lunch. Bookstores and restaurants packed the pedestrian mall north of the lake. Grady examined menus. One offered kangaroo steak but he passed it up picturing the poor animals hit by cars. In the square a mime knight did mock battle with a man in a rhinoceros suit. Grady wished he'd brought his father's camera. He got an outdoor table at a Vietnamese place and had a passable duck with broken rice.

After lunch Grady explored the Australian National Museum and found an Aboriginal painting of dots, animal shapes, and wavy lines. The crescents were the shapes people leave in the dirt after sitting. He learned that Australians refer to all native peoples as Aborigines and their own as Aboriginal People of Aboriginals. Despite the Aboriginals having lived in Australia for fifty thousand years, the arriving Europeans referred to the land as *terra nullius*, meaning no one's land or land free for the taking. Grady entered a reproduction of a nineteenth-century clapboard church and sat in one of the pews.

"Our God is a good God," the recorded preacher's voice said from a hidden speaker.

Grady could almost see him standing with a black, leather-bound bible in front of a sea of brown faces speaking his message out of concern or maybe just to make the conquered people more docile.

In the courtyard children walked on a map of Australia made of rubberized tiles. Grady joined them, visiting the places he wouldn't get to see on this trip – Perth, Darwin, Brisbane, and the red center.

He left the museum, crossed the lake, and explored the manicured lawn of the park surrounding Capitol Hill. In the background the sleek, new Parliament House, with its sloping roof and silver spire, stood like a rocket ship visiting from the future. A ramshackle collection of tents clustered in front of the older building it replaced. This was the Aboriginal Tent Embassy, formed to protest the government's treatment of its native people. A limp, red-and-black flag with a yellow circle in its center hung over a sign asking for donations. Grady dropped a two-dollar coin in the bucket before crossing the bridge again. He lounged in the Anzac Park until dusk. Then he returned to the motel. When Grady got back to the room, his father was sitting in the dark while the TV showed a rugby game. Three empty cans of beer sat on the table. Earl nursed the fourth.

"You want to get some dinner, dad?"

"Not hungry."

"Well, I'm going to go." Grady looked in his suitcase but failed to find a clean shirt. "Did you do the laundry?"

"Guess it must be about time to put the clothes in the dryer." Earl struggled to his feet and stumbled toward the door.

"I'll do it." Grady scooped some coins off the table and stepped outside.

He located the laundry room and found that a frustrated guest had unloaded their wet clothing from the washer hours before and placed it atop a dryer. Grady fed coins into the dryer, put the clothes inside, and went for a sandwich at a nearby pub. When he returned to the room, his father was asleep.

In the following days Grady coaxed his father out for a walk around the university and a few brief museum visits but Earl always went back to the motel room for more drinking. In one sense it was a relief. His father's company felt as constricting as the pullover sweater he had worn when he was seven. On one night Earl had already had a few beers by the time he and Grady walked to dinner. The pub had opened its big shutters to let in the temperate air of the Australian summer. Some customers sat at wooden tables on the patio right off the gravel parking lot. Inside a man with a muscular build and short-cropped hair tended bar and took food orders, chosen from a menu chalked on a blackboard. Grady and his father ordered fish and chips with coleslaw. Earl got yet another beer to drink. They looked for a free table.

"How about that one?" Grady yelled to be heard over the crowd.

Earl set down his glass and beer slopped over the rim onto the table's scruffy surface. Grady collected the plastic baskets and dirty napkins, left by the previous diners, and carried them to the trash. The acrid smell of cigarette smoke seemed to follow him back to the table. It came from three college-aged women chain-smoking Craven A's at the table behind Earl. All had hourglass figures and dressed in the styles one would expect in a cigarette ad.

"It just kills me to see a young woman like you ruining her health like that," Earl told the brunette who wore her green-tinted hair piled like a Mayan headdress.

The woman sighed. Her friend, a blonde whose thin neck conflicted with the rugged image of her jeans and thick-soled shoes, rolled her eyes.

"I mean, my wife was a smoker too. I just cremated her last week. Cancer. Got her ashes back in the motel room."

"Dad." Grady kicked Earl under the table.

"Sorry to hear that," said the woman with a chin shaped like a dumpling.

"Can I buy you girls a drink?" Earl asked.

"No thanks." The blonde replied in less than a millisecond.

"Come on!" Earl voice grew loud. "One little drink won't kill you."

"Dad!"

The women gathered their glasses and moved to a different table. The room grew quiet. Grady felt eyes turn toward him. A man with a hatchet-shaped nose and equally deadly looking fists seemed especially interested. If only Grady's father would shut the hell up.

"Sorry," Grady said. "He hasn't been himself since my mom died."

Grady looked toward the counter. With his eyes he implored the bartender to help. The man nodded and disappeared into the kitchen. He came back with two takeout bags moments later.

"Order's up, mate."

"Come on, dad." Grady picked up the food from the counter and escorted the cause of his shame out.

The laughter, he expected to erupt behind them, never materialized. Serenaded by cicadas, Grady and Earl ate by the motel pool. Earl turned in and Grady remained outside looking at the stars.

The next morning they woke up late and had breakfast. Earl seemed to have no memory of the previous night. He showed no interest in moving on. Grady let him be. They stayed for a week. After checking out of the motel on what was to be their last day, Grady and Earl drove to the top of Black Mountain and took the elevator to the observation deck of the Telstra Tower where Earl snapped photos of the view below. They took a short hike and stopped for dinner in town before getting on the highway.

Their plan was to head north to the Hume Highway at Yassi. The driving started out well. Grady had grown more confident behind the wheel and had navigated traffic heading out of Canberra without expecting a catastrophe any time he changed lanes. Earl occupied himself by listening to the news on the radio until the station faded into static with distance. The sun set which was fine with Grady. At night there would be fewer cars on the road and the driving would be more pleasant.

"What do you think about a brief stop back in Macau after we leave here?" Earl asked.

"Why?"

"I think we let the casinos off too easy."

"Weren't we going to New Zealand?"

An oncoming car approached and Grady turned down his high beams.

"Just a thought. Could win some money for your college fund." Earl paused. "You know, the University of Nebraska has a really good reputation."

"I don't want to go there."

"Why are you so set on Washington when you don't even know what your major's going to be and what the faculty offers?"

"They have lots of good teachers." Grady turned on the radio to drown out his father but all he got was static.

"You're just following that girl. Hell, you probably won't even care about her in a year." Earl turned the radio off. "You're going to face a really tough job climate after you graduate so you'd better be prepared. When I went to college, I knew what I wanted to do and chose the best school for it."

"Worked out well for you. Didn't it?"

"Don't talk to me that way, Grady!" Earl's face glowed like that of an angry ghost in the dashboard's blue light. "I'm your father."

"Well, I don't have to go to Washington. I just know I'm not going to Omaha."

Grady was about to bring up Earl's visit to the Dutch prostitute when a shadow scuttled across the road. He slammed on the brakes and felt the thud of the car colliding with the scurrying creature.

"See what you made me do!" Grady jammed the gearshift into park before the car stopped rolling.

It jerked to a stop. Grady jumped out and circled to the front. Blood and fur stuck to the dented bumper and the left headlight was broken. Grady walked back along the road to where a large, woodchuck-like animal lay still with a huge gash in its head.

"Looks like we found your mother's wombat," Earl said from behind Grady's shoulder.

Grady stared at the dark pool of blood on the pavement. He wanted to cover up this murder, just drag the carcass into the bushes and go but he couldn't bring himself to touch it. If only someone could get him out of this mess! A white station wagon pulled over and illuminated them with its halogen headlights.

"Need a hand?" the driver asked. He was a dark-haired man with weathered skin and bushy eyebrows.

"We hit an animal," Grady said.

"Is that so?" The driver got out of his vehicle and squatted next to the dead animal. "She's a female. Did you check for joeys?"

"For what?"

The stranger probed the animal's belly, reached into her pouch, and removed a pink, hairless creature the size of his fist. With its nose and long ears the baby wombat's face resembled an aardvark's. He mewed and scratched with his front claws as the stranger held him to his shoulder.

"There you go, little fellow." He turned to Grady. "You have a towel to keep him warm?"

Grady stared.

"A cloth or something?"

"Sure." Grady opened the trunk and returned with an old T-shirt.

"Thanks, mate." The stranger wrapped the joey in the cloth and handed him to Earl while he made a call on his cell phone. "Yeah, hi. We rescued a joey from an injured wombat up on the Barton Highway about twenty kilometers south of Yassi. Is there anywhere I can drop him off? No, he doesn't appear to be hurt. All right." He put his hand over the mouthpiece. "It's the RSPCA. They're checking on a wildlife carer to take him," he whispered. "Hello. Okay. We've got to go to Canberra, then." He wrote on a scrap of paper. "Will do. Thanks." He hung up.

"What did they say?" Earl asked.

"I think we got a place." The stranger made another phone call and got directions. He hung up the phone and clipped it to his belt. "You mind taking him? If I'm late, my wife will kill me."

"We'll take him," Earl said. "It's the least we can do."

The stranger gave them directions, wished them luck, and continued on his way. Earl carried the baby wombat to the car, held the creature in his lap, and stroked its head to quiet its squeals while Grady made a three-point turn to head back the way they'd come. When he cut the wheel hard left he heard the tire rub against the wheel well.

"I don't think they'll ever rent a car to us again in this country," Grady said.

Earl was too busy cooing at the joey to respond, not that he'd showed much interest in driving in Australia, anyway. It took an hour to reach Canberra and another to find the wildlife carer's house. The wooden, one-story structure with a backyard surrounded by a chain-link fence was located on a large unkempt property on one of the winding roads that covered Black Mountain, not far from where they'd spent the afternoon. A single bulb lit the front porch. Grady parked the car. He and Earl approached to door via the concrete walkway.

"You the ones who called earlier?" asked the thin woman who answered the door.

She must have been stunning in her day. Despite the sun damage and well-earned laugh lines, her face was still attractive. Her tight jeans with faded back pockets highlighted her slender figure to good effect. Long, corn-silk hair hung over her shoulders to the level of her apricot-sized breasts.

"That's us," Earl said.

"Well, someone called for us," Grady added.

"You'd better bring it inside, then."

They entered. The sound of a TV came from the living room. Sandals, running shoes, and a muddy pair of lace-up boots sprawled on the shoe rack. A gangly, young kangaroo hopped into the hallway and nuzzled the woman's hand.

"Not now, Tippy." She pushed the marsupial's muzzle away. "Can't you see we have company?"

She led Grady and Earl through the kitchen and into a den that was closed off by a waist-high metal screen. The legs of the table and chairs showed splintered wood as if they'd been chewed.

"Let's have a look, then," the woman said.

The joey began squirming and squealing as soon he left Earl's hands.

"What are you doing?" the woman crooned and tickled the animal's jaw as she unwrapped the cloth from his body. "Doesn't seem to be injured. You feed him anything?"

"No," Earl said.

"Good. Most people think they're doing them a favor by giving them cow's milk. Gives them diarrhea." The joey stretched a paw toward her face and the woman brushed it away. "You behave yourself!" She placed the animal in a cloth pouch hanging from a peg on the wall and retrieved a baby bottle from the kitchen.

The joey began to feed from the nipple.

"You're from the States, then?" the woman asked.

"Uh huh."

"What do you do when you're not running down little critters?"

"Don't be too hard on the boy," Earl said. "He's not used to driving on the left."

"I know how hard that is," the woman said. "I went to Los Angeles and rented a car. Thought I'd nearly die. I'm Janice by the way. Janice MacKenzie."

"I'm Earl and this is my son, Grady."

"We're taking a year off to see the world." Grady glared at his father who was grinning like a chimpanzee.

"Oh, is your wife traveling with you, too?" Janice asked.

An open-mouthed look of confusion replaced Earl's smile.

"Your ring." Janice pointed to Earl's left hand.

"My mother died," Grady said.

"Sorry." Janice's expression melted into a mask of concern. "Would you like a cup of tea?"

"I'd love one," Earl said.

"Have you tried Scientology?" Janice stepped into the kitchen and filled the teapot with water.

"No, what's that about?" Earl followed her.

Grady couldn't believe it. Rowan wasn't even dead two weeks and already his horn-dog father was chasing skirts.

"Dad, we really need to get going."

"Do you have any adults?" Earl asked Janice.

"Adults?"

"Adult wombats. Before my wife died, I promised her we'd see one."

"No adults. Soon as they get older, I move them to another carer's closer to the bush." She set the kettle down. "I have a juvenile out back, though. Want to see her?"

"I'd love to," Earl said. "We tried to see one in the Sydney zoo but he was hiding in a log."

"They do that." The woman led them into the backyard.

From the dirt piled around the corrugated-steel-lined animal enclosure, Grady guessed it extended several feet underground.

"Come on out, Crackers." The woman knelt by the open end of a concrete pipe that emerged from a mound of dirt.

The wombat ambled out of her den and peered with tiny eyes on both sides of her tennis-ball-sized nose. Her bear-shaped body was the size of a small dog. With a wedge-shaped head, powerful forelegs, and inch-long claws she was built for digging as evidenced by the dirt on her brown coat.

"That's a good wombat." Janice scratched Crackers behind the ear.

Crackers showed her appreciation by pawing a furrow in the ground.

"That's the cutest animal I've ever seen in my life." Earl took a step forward.

"You want to say hi to our guests, Crackers?" The woman hefted the animal onto her lap and stood supporting Crackers with an arm under her rump.

Crackers protested this indignity by waving her stubby forelegs in the air. Earl reached out. Crackers blinked each time he pat her head. Grady came forward from the patio, extended a tentative hand, and stroked the animal. Her fur felt like a steel brush. Crackers began to squirm and Janice set her down. After a final look at the humans, the wombat turned and disappeared into her burrow.

"Do you think the little guy will be okay?" Earl asked as they stepped inside.

"Won't know for a couple of days," Janice said. "He's eating and that's a good sign. You've got my number. Give me a call in a week and I'll let you know how he's doing."

Grady and Earl left. It was too late to get back on the highway so they returned to the motel. Earl wiggled the wedding ring off his finger and went right to bed. Grady stayed up watching TV. There was the usual talk about Iraq on the news. He switched channels to a rerun of *Law and Order*. By the time A.D.A. Jack McCoy outmaneuvered the sleazy defense lawyer to put the murdering daughter in law away for good, Grady's eyes had grown heavy.

He turned out the light and crawled into bed but anxiety banged shelves and stomped around the second floor of his consciousness. Was there going to be money for college after this trip? First the old man was going to buy him a house. The he tried to send Grady to Omaha to cut costs. Damn his mother, anyway! If she hadn't smoked herself to death, he wouldn't be halfway around the world in a stinking motel room with his boozy old man. Sure was a cute wombat, though. It was too hot. Grady stripped off his T-shirt and went to the bathroom. He returned to bed and eventually fell into a fitful sleep.

A shaft of light coming through a gap in the curtains woke him. Earl was still asleep so Grady dressed in the bathroom and tiptoed out the door. With his nerves raw from his late night, he was unprepared for the daylight's assault. How would he ever stay alert during the drive to Melbourne? Grady took a deep breath and stood straighter. He had to make it somehow in order to discourage his father from drinking with a heavy schedule of sightseeing and activities. Maybe a zoo or wild animal park would be good. Food would keep him awake. Grady walked to the convenience store on the corner and bought orange juice, a package of chocolate donuts, and a chicken sandwich.

Even at the early hour, the merciless sun barraged the streets with heat. By the time Grady got back to the motel, his shirt was sticky with sweat. He decided to eat outside and let his father sleep. On the way to his seat by the pool he stopped by the rental car, walked around the driver's side, and squatted by the damaged headlight. A pool of bright green radiator fluid had formed under the engine.

"Shit!"

They wouldn't be going anywhere, today. Grady sighed. He'd have to tell the old man but he'd do it after breakfast. With a hand braced on the hot, metal hood Grady heaved himself to his feet. He walked to the pool and sat on a deck chair to eat before delivering the bad news.

They retrieved Rowan's suitcase from the trunk and hauled it to the room before the tow truck came to haul the car away. Despite Earl's pleas over the phone, the agent at Avis refused to rent him another. Word had gotten around. Earl's inquiries at other rental car agencies met with similar refusals. This didn't seem to bother Earl whose travel ambitions had shrunk to a walk to the convenience store for more beer.

Grady was itching to get out of the motel. He wandered around the parks, had a late dinner, and returned after sunset. The room was dark. No doubt Earl was out getting something to eat or more likely something to drink. Grady unlocked the door, stepped inside, and reached for the light switch.

There was a frantic rustling of covers in his father's bed. Grady caught a glimpse of breast before Janice, the wildlife carer, managed to cover her naked body. She and Earl flushed with embarrassment.

"Jesus!" Grady slammed the door on his way out. So much for his father's love of animals!

Earl did not speak about his encounter. They languished in Canberra for a few more days before Grady realized they could take a bus to Melbourne. To make their luggage lighter they spread Rowan's personal effects on the motel room floor and separated her possessions into three piles: those to keep, donate to charity, and throw away. Lipstick, mascara, the hated cigarettes, and those lotions that promised youthful skin but delivered only the cloying stench of industrial perfume went into the trash. So too did the feminine products – a half-used box of tampons and a beige plastic case similar to the one Marisol used to store her diaphragm. Rowan's medications weren't there. Perhaps the police had removed them.

In death his mother had no privacy. Lacy bras and panties, even some thongs went into the pile destined for the Salvation Army. Pants, skirts, running shoes, and blouses (some stained with sweat) joined them. The thought of Rowan's purple sweater-vest lying unwanted in some clothing bin broke Grady's heart. He placed it in the pile of keepsakes.

She had two books: Sylvia Plath's *Ariel* and *Super System*. These were kept. The jar of small coins used in their weekly poker games was judged too heavy and consigned to the donation pile (as if the Australians had any use for foreign pennies).

They kept Rowan's documents: her recent passport, social security card, and the California driver's license with its picture taken long before Rowan had lost her hair to chemotherapy. This was how Grady wanted to remember her. She'd carried photo of him too, from back when he was a gawky seven-year-old with bangs growing over his eyebrows. In one picture he held a radio-controlled model airplane, a P 51 Mustang that he and his dad had assembled and would soon shatter against a tree trunk on its maiden flight. Rowan's wedding ring and necklace, the silver Celtic knot, went into the keep pile.

Grady looked at the keepsakes. All that remained of his mother's life were a few documents, some clothing, and pieces of jewelry. Now he was really alone. Who would know him as she did? Who would he go to for a kind word and home-baked butter cookie when conflict brought him to tears like the time he quit the softball team out of frustration with the coach? Not Earl. Definitely not Earl. With both Rowan and Marisol gone, life had banished him from the comfort of loving arms, banished him to the cold iron-and-concrete world of men. He snatched the necklace and fastened it around his neck. A sob began to thicken his throat. Before it could erupt, he stood and stuffed the donation pile into Rowan's bag.

"I'll take it." Grady zipped the bag up and carried it out the door.

He rolled the suitcase down the sidewalk toward town. Its wheels roared against the concrete and made a double click every time they crossed a seam. Grady hadn't written down the Salvation Army's address but he couldn't go back. He might find it in a phone book but he didn't see a pay phone. The sound of cars whizzing past grated as if rubbing his nerves with sandpaper. He walked on despite the summer heat sapping his strength as if he were moving through Jell-O.

When he reached downtown, Grady dragged the purple bag off the main road and onto side streets. It followed him like a stalking dingo as he searched the trendy shops for a thrift store. A South

Asian proprietor, standing outside his camera shop, gave Grady a kind but puzzled look. It would have been sensible to stop and ask to use the phone book but Grady walked on and eventually crossed the bridge to Capitol Hill.

The Parliament House's guards did not extend their patrols to the Aboriginal Tent Embassy. If they had, they would have surely searched the purple bag. Instead the first man to glimpse inside was an Aboriginal who stepped out of his tent as Grady arrived. He had dark skin, a broad nose, and a chin that made his face look like it was in a permanent scowl.

"Can you use this stuff?" Grady let go of the handle and let it drop at the Aboriginal's feet.

The man unzipped the case and held up a turquoise blouse.

"You sure you want to get rid of these?" Wrinkles formed on the Aboriginal's forehead.

Grady's frustration moved faster than the man's puzzled thoughts. Why did everything have to be so goddamned difficult?

"Just keep it. All right?" Grady walked away before the Aboriginal could protest.

The next day Grady and his father boarded the crowded bus to Melbourne. Matching their seat numbers to those on their tickets Grady was dismayed to learn their places were next to the bathroom. During the eight-hour journey Grady stared at the scenery while trying to ignore both Earl and the sickly sweet smell of the toilet bowl disinfectant. Could it get any worse? Almost without thinking he reached into a bag of cheese curls and popped one in his mouth. What the hell was he doing? He set the bag down in disgust. After six months of travel he was developing a paunch around his middle. He was getting soft. From now on things would be different. No more sleeping late, fatty meals, and beer. He needed to find an aikido dojo and do some serious training.

They got in late and took a room in a hotel on the south bank of the Yarra River. Before unpacking Grady rifled the phone book, found a nearby dojo, and scribbled the address on a notepad by the phone.

The next morning they ate breakfast at a bakery. Grady had two whole-grain muffins and juice while Earl consumed sugary donuts. Grady badgered his father into exploring the surreal architecture of

Federation Square with its buildings' crazy, silver rhomboid shapes and view of the nineteenth-century train station. Earl took a few pictures but even a running shoe the size of a Honda Civic didn't please him as much as the numbing comfort of the hotel bar.

Grady was on his own. Carrying the gi he hadn't worn since Amsterdam, he wandered the downtown pedestrian mall, visited a museum, and eventually ate dinner at a food stall in the Victoria Market.

At 6:00, Grady set off toward the dojo by walking east to Nicholson Street and turning left. A green streetcar pulled to a stop and a half-dozen passengers boarded. Grady could have done the same but was unsure of the price and procedure so he let the streetcar pull away. The walk would do him good. After all, the dojo was only a few inches away on the map.

Past the park, Grady walked by Indian and Thai restaurants, vegetarian places, CD shops, and punk used clothing stores with black facades decorated with skulls. A half-hour later, the street branched into a Y and he was only an inch closer to his goal on the map. He picked up his pace until the muscles in his calves filled with lactic acid and complained with a dull, leaden burn. Another streetcar pulled to a stop. This time Grady wouldn't let it get away.

"Will this take me to Kenton Street?" Grady asked the driver, an olive-skinned man in a light blue uniform shirt.

"Yes." The driver's middle-eastern accent seemed flavored with honey, yogurt, rosemary, and lamb.

Grady boarded, plundered his pockets for coins to pay the fare, and sat behind two enormous women with overflowing shopping bags at their feet.

"Did you try that conditioner Shelly recommended?"

"Didn't help. With this frightful humidity my hair looks like a steel wool scrubber."

Grady tuned their conversation out to rehearse his visit to the dojo in his mind. After the events of the past weeks he needed some kind of victory and this would be it. With his right hand he made a palm-up motions as if hooking a punch with the knob of his thumb, rotated his hand palm down, closed his fist, and extended his arm while imagining taking his opponent to the mat. Yeah, that's what he needed, something hard and fast! Images of action and excitement played in his mind. He felt the wild, *ki* energy expanding from his *hara* like the shockwave from a nuclear blast.

"Kenton Street." The driver stopped and pulled the silver crank to open the doors.

Grady left via the rear exit, spotted the Japanese characters for aikido (harmony, energy, path) on the dojo's sign, and entered. A willowy woman in a white T-shirt and baggy, olive drab combat pants stood by the door and lifted wispy, blonde hair off her neck to let the fan cool her skin. Grady had entered the paradise of aiki-nymphs! There were other attractive babes too! One, with thick black hair done in braids, left the changing room. Her blue eyes looked at the world in childlike wonder from behind wire-rimmed glasses. He would have given anything to be the soft, gray fabric of her running bra that snuggled her torso under her gi top.

"Excuse me." The woman in the army pants brushed past breaking Grady's chain of thought.

Grady introduced himself to the teacher, a slight man with a stringy mustache that grew over his lip, paid the ten-dollar mat fee, and changed into his gi. As soon as the class had bowed in and completed the warm-ups, Grady knew coming had been a mistake. The instructor had them practice downward open-handed chops as if they were a real attack that wouldn't result in shattering their metacarpals on their opponent's skull. He'd stumbled into a class of what Wakayama Sensei called wimp aikido whose adherents groove on energy while ignoring all martial aspects of the art. Grady looked at the door but there was no face-saving escape. He was stuck for the hour.

It got worse. When the teacher demonstrated a *nikyo* from a collar grab, he stared at the grasping hand ignoring his opponent's other fist, a beginner's mistake. Didn't he know he could get hit?

One of the beautiful girls bowed to Grady. When she reached for his collar, Grady stepped to the outside with a simulated strike, brushed his hand down her warm rosy forearm, placed her hand on his shoulder, and inched into a wristlock.

"Too rough," she said.

Grady held his tongue. In his home dojo a black belt would have said, "This is a fighting art, you know," but here Grady was a guest. He treated her like a tray of champagne glasses until it was time to change partners. The minute hand crawled toward the hour. Grady gritted his teeth when the instructor left the wooden dagger in his attacker's hand after taking the man down from a knife thrust. That kind of thing could get you killed! Then, mercifully the class ended. Grady dashed into the men's changing room, put on his street clothes, and made for the exit. The woman in the combat pants intercepted him.

"So, what part of the States are you from, then?" On closer inspection her teeth were crooked and her eyes slightly crossed giving her a feral, wanton look.

"California." Grady reached for his shoes.

"My last boyfriend was from California." She flapped the fabric of her T-shirt to pump cool air next to her velvety skin. "Don't you just love Sensei Coolbreeze? He's teaching tomorrow night, too. See you then?"

God, she was lovely. The wheels and gears in Grady's mind turned. All he'd have to do was put up with another hour but he just couldn't.

"No, I won't be in town that long." Grady slipped out the door leaving the aiki-nymph's mouth pursed into a rosebud of disappointment.

The streetcar came to a stop, he boarded, and the driver pulled away. Grady looked back at the dojo and pictured the woman's streamlined body.

"I'm such a fucking idiot!" he muttered.

He'd started the evening with visions of triumph but how could you have victory without a worthwhile opponent? It wasn't fair! He never had a chance to show what he could do at that silly dojo. There was a lesson in this. You had to give people the opportunity to try. Then, it hit him. Triumph? The opportunity to compete? Who had he denied the chance to try?

The suspension rumbled as the streetcar slowed at Grady's stop. He left by the rear exit and walked west. Tourists and backpackers milled about on the streets near the domed railroad station. In the distance yellow, sodium lights glowed on the bridge that spanned the Yarra River. Grady picked up his pace hoping to catch his father while he was still sober.

CHAPTER 13

Earl had to spend hours yelling on the phone before the airline let them use their round-the-world tickets to return. It helped that he and Grady were flying to Macau not Hong Kong so technically they weren't backtracking. Once their plane touched down, they wasted little time. After checking in at the hotel, they dropped their bags in the room. Earl removed traveler's checks from his money belt and handed it to Grady.

"Remember what we talked about, son. No matter how much I beg, don't give me any more."

"Right." Grady wrapped Earl's money belt over the one he already wore and left his shirt untucked to camouflage the bulge. All that cash would make him a good score for some lucky mugger but Grady wouldn't go far. He figured he'd spot the old man an extra thousand dollars if it came to it. They'd have to eat fast food for weeks but it would be worth it to put an end to his father's moping.

They took the elevator to the lobby and crossed the courtyard to the casino where Earl exchanged his traveler's checks for poker chips. Then he strode past the beeping slot machines that filled the air with dissonance and picked up his pace once they got to the roulette wheels. Grady completely lost sight of his father near the Baccarat tables but he knew where his father was going. Once Grady entered the poker room, he found Earl scouting tables.

"It's beautiful. Isn't it?"

"I guess." Grady thought back to his pockmarked algebra teacher who'd said the only surefire way to win at gambling was not to play.

"Want to play, too?"

"Okay." Grady accepted a fraction of his father's chips and sat.

"Welcome to the game," said a tall Chinese man with a horse-like face.

The dealer withdrew a fresh deck of cards from the recessed black box in front of him, shuffled, and dealt. Grady fumbled to lift the corners of his two cards off the green baize.

"Thirty dollars to call, sir," the dealer said.

Thirty dollars. That was thirty Hong Kong dollars, about four dollars US. Grady still had Earl's money belt but doubted he'd be tempted to dip into the cash inside. This was his mother's passion, not his. He had an unsuited Ten and Jack. Grady pushed three beige chips forward. A Caucasian guy with shoulder-length hair raised. Earl folded and so did Grady.

Despite all his practice with his mom, the cards came too fast for Grady to keep up. After losing a third of his chips to the longhaired guy in a game of chicken, he reverted to defensive mode, only betting when he had an outstanding hand or when he was a blind. Earl won a pot and tipped the dealer a chip. How had he gotten so good all of a sudden? Had he been bluffing during all those Sunday-night poker games?

The dealer returned the deck into the recessed black box, got a fresh one, and dealt. Grady had two Queens. He pushed forward three chips.

"You're not helping me, Chen," the longhaired guy mucked his cards.

The dealer burned a card from the deck and turned over three cards for the flop. One was another Queen. Grady bet another six chips. The players saw through him and folded. The dealer pushed the meager pot his way. The chips he'd won didn't replace those lost to the blind bets that kept bleeding him. Earl won another hand. He seemed to have more chips than when he'd started but not as many as the longhaired guy or the old woman in the turquoise jersey. Grady couldn't get it together. Dizzy from too much concentration on an empty stomach, he looked at his tiny stack of chips and decided to quit.

"I'm out. Thanks for the game." Grady went to the cashier's window and exchanged his chips.

He left the casino and ate dinner at a small, family-run café with cheap, stainless-steel teapots on the tables and a big-screen TV playing shows from Hong Kong. After a meal of deep-fried tofu and vegetables in brown sauce, he stayed to watch a kung fu program. He didn't understand the Cantonese but enjoyed the fight scenes between guys in period costumes and wigs.

When Grady returned to the casino, his father wasn't in the poker room. After searching the other floors, Grady went back to the hotel room and found his father lying in his underwear atop one of the twin beds. The TV was showing a commercial for some cleaning product.

"Dad? Do you need more money?"

"No, I won six hundred bucks."

"How come you stopped?"

"It was just no good."

"Okay," Grady said his words slowly. "I'm going to take a shower."

Inside the bathroom, Grady took off his shirt and removed Earl's money belt. Curious about its thickness, he unzipped it and found nineteen hundred dollars in cash as well as plane tickets and traveler's checks. Grady ran his fingers over the crisp paper. There's nothing like the feel of new banknotes, especially those sporting portraits of Ben Franklin and Ulysses S. Grant. With all the drinking and gambling, his father would never notice if some were missing. And anyway, Earl was so erratic that it would be better to hold some backup cash for him. At least, that's what Grady told himself. He took eight hundred dollars and returned the rest.

Grady woke before his father the next morning, tiptoed out of the room, and walked downtown for breakfast. There was no hurry. The old man would probably sleep until noon. The sun was shining and the air was balmy. Grady realized Thanksgiving had already passed, not that he had much to be thankful for. Rather than eat in a restaurant, he bought a box of malted soymilk and some pastries called greasy sticks, which resembled the *churros* in Spain. He found a seat on a bench in the square and performed the small, soymilk ceremony he'd always enjoyed. Grady stripped the prophylactic coating off the straw and stabbed its sharp end into the circle of aluminum foil on the box top. Then expecting the soymilk to be cold like the others he'd had, he brought the straw to his lips. The soymilk was warm. Bizarre!

He spent the morning browsing shop windows and learned Macao had the best almond cookies, crispy, golden, and not too sweet. Mainland China was close. Across a mile of water, the windows of its high-rise apartments stared like hundreds of spying eyes. Recalling how many refugees swam these waters to escape, he wondered what went on behind the buildings' facades.

That afternoon Earl took him to lunch at a restaurant with brush paintings on the walls and fish with heads that resembled penises swimming in a tank by the door. The hostess sat them at a table by the window. Grady opened the menu.

"Jeez! These meals are like a hundred bucks!"

"We're not going to live forever. Might as well enjoy life while we can. Why don't we start with the shark fin soup and follow it with Peking duck?"

Grady looked at the menu. The prices for those weren't even listed.

"You sure? They're real expensive."

"What did I tell you?" Earl held up his index finger.

"Enjoy life while I can."

"That's right."

After taking their order the waiter spread napkins on their laps. He returned moments later with a bottle of wine. Earl sniffed the cork and nodded.

"This lunch comes in the way of an apology." Earl sipped his wine. "I was wrong to pressure you into going to Nebraska. I realize that now. You've got a honey in Seattle and I'm sure you're eager to get back to her. How is Marisol, anyway?"

"She left me for another guy."

"I'm sorry, Grady but I can't say I didn't see it coming. Let me give you a little hard-won advice. Women are unreliable and a man's got to have a backup plan."

"By backup plan you mean…"

"You've got to be like a pool player, always scoping out your next shot. Of course if you can knock in two balls at once so much the better."

The waiter brought a tureen of soup. Earl waited for him to ladle it into bowls before continuing.

"Look, for women sex is a weapon. They'll play with your emotions like a cat if you let them. Until you find the right one, you need a backup plan so you can bail whenever they become impossible."

"Backup plan." Grady's mouth formed a smile. The words felt smooth as the wine on his tongue.

"If I were you, I'd be chasing tail in every country I visited. You see some of the honeys around here?"

The waiter brought a tray piled with duck and demonstrated how to top a pancake with plum sauce, skin, and green onion. Grady wasn't sure how he felt listening to Earl talk about sex. He was flattered that his father was treating him like an adult but it was also a little like eating raw octopus. After they finished the duck, the waiter brought a dessert of sesame balls, pounded rice surrounding sweetened sesame paste and topped with grated coconut. The check arrived on a lacquer tray.

"Grady, why don't you wait outside while I deal with this?" Earl put on his reading glasses to examine the numbers.

What a strange request! Earl had never asked him to leave a restaurant before. Grady exited through the glass door and stood in the flow of pedestrians, feeling like an ant on the Indianapolis speedway. He ducked closer to the wall to get out of the way of a man carrying a stack of white boxes.

"Let's go!" Earl rushed outside.

"You! Come back!" The waiter dashed after him.

Dodging pedestrians like a skier through slalom poles, Grady sprinted after his father who moved pretty fast for an old guy. Grady poured on the speed pumping his legs for all he was worth and sucking air through his mouth as exhaustion burned in his chest. They skidded around a corner and jogged right at an intersection.

"We lost him!" Earl bent over panting and began to laugh. "Did you see that son of a bitch?"

"You didn't pay?"

"At those prices? Three hundred American dollars for lunch? It's bullshit!" Earl straightened up. "Bastards will rip you off any way they can. You know what else is a ripoff? Fucking hotel mini bars. I'm going back to the room." Earl handed Grady fifty dollars. "Do me a favor, sport. Pick me up some wine."

CHAPTER 14

gsankyu@hotmail.com
Dear Marisol,

How are you? I'm doing pretty well considering that my mom passed away in Australia. I know you liked her and would want to know. She went peacefully with both dad and me in the room. We had a simple ceremony afterwards.

My dad and I spent Christmas in Auckland, New Zealand. It's really bizarre having Xmas decorations up in the summer down here. Hope things are OK with you.

Grady

OBgrrl@yahoo.com
Dear Grady,

I'm so sorry about your mom. You must be heartbroken being all alone so far from home. Let me know if I can do anything.

Marisol

gsankyu@hotmail.com
Dear Marisol,

We're doing fine. Hard as it was my mother's passing brought my father and me closer. There's a lot of strength in family. Don't you think?

They're getting ready for New Year's Eve here. I'm optimistic. With all that's happened, the next year is bound to be a good one.

Grady

At 9:00 PM on New Year's Eve, Grady entered the aikido dojo, took off his shoes, and approached a young man who was tying a *hakama* around his hips.

"Excuse me, Sensei. I train with Wakayama Sensei in California. Would it be okay for me to join your class, tonight?"

"What's your name?"

"Grady. Grady Evans."

"Welcome and good on ya." With his blonde curls and oversized judogi top, the teacher resembled a boy in his father's shirt. "Tonight we have *toshikoshi keiko*. We'll train until just after midnight and then have a little cake to celebrate the New Year."

"Is there a mat fee?"

"Naw. Changing room's that way."

After changing into his gi, Grady bowed, stepped onto the green tatami mat, and stretched while watching the other students. Two practiced *shiho nage*, a thin man with long sideburns swung a heavy *bokken*, and a stocky woman in a black *hakama* knelt and stretched her wrists. Grady did a few rolls. It had been a while and he'd developed a few corners that made him feel like a square wheel. The class was mostly a review of techniques he already knew, *sankyo*, *iriminage*, and the like. The aerobic workout got his blood flowing and he sweated the poisons out of his system. His training partners were easy to work with. There were no wrist-crunching sadists or six-hundred-pound gorillas muscling through atrocious technique.

From time to time, he glanced at the clock and grew more nervous as it swept toward midnight. It would be great to stay for the party and compare notes with his fellow trainees but how could he leave his father alone on New Year's Eve? As the minute hand swept toward 11:00, he made a decision. Soon the teacher called a break.

"Sensei, I'd love to stay for the rest of the class but my father's all alone. I think I need to go and keep him company."

"No worries. Come back any time."

Grady took the bus back to the apartment he'd found for them on the K Road. Inside Earl was sitting in an easy chair and watching an Australian movie channel. One hand balanced a beer perched on the armrest. Three empties lay at his feet.

"Dad, do you want to go celebrate New Year's Eve?"

Earl squinted like a far-sighted man trying to read a newspaper an inch from his nose. He'd stopped shaving and his beard had grown.

"Nah, I don't want to deal with the crowds."

"All right, then. I'm going out for a bit. Will you be okay?"

Earl turned back to the TV until Grady reached the door.

"Will you get me another beer?" Earl crumpled the empty and dropped it on the carpet.

Grady walked east on the K Road negotiating the partiers who'd overflowed the bars onto the sidewalk until he reached Queen Street. There, the authorities had blocked off traffic in favor of pedestrians. Much like a drop of mercury coalescing into another in chem. lab, Grady joined the flow of the crowd. He didn't want to be distinguishable. On this night he wanted to be part of the human family.

Aotea Square was barricaded for some ticketed event. A band had just played the final chords in its set, and the audience left their seats to find bathrooms and snacks. Grady rode the surge of Asians, turbaned Sikhs, tattooed Maoris, and Caucasians past the giant Santa Claus that stood like a horrible genetic mutation from a 1950s A-bomb movie.

"Fucking bitch!" A woman swung a purse at a trophy blonde in a blue dress. The two clashed like sumo wrestlers in press-on nails until their boyfriends dragged them apart.

You'd have to be insane, a cab driver, or possibly an insane cab driver to drive on a night like this. Despite that fact, cars packed the streets around the Sky Tower. After crossing the crowded road, Grady found a place with a good view in a parking lot. The husband of an Indian couple, next to him, pointed his cell-phone camera at the tower while his sari-wearing wife held hands with their daughters. The sound of broken glass came from down the street. Grady smelled cigarettes.

The fireworks started with the usual foreplay around midnight. A rocket flew from the tower and burst into a glowing starfish. The crowd went, "Ooh." This continued until the display ended with an orgasm of sound and color. All the excitement made Grady hungry so he dispensed with the resolution phase and walked to a McDonalds where the uniformed guard at the entrance nodded to him. His shake and Quarter Pounder (no Royale with Cheese here) tasted just like those back home.

"Happy New Year," Grady said to the women at the next table.

"Same to you." She had three inches of bracelets on her wrists and wore nothing under her leather vest.

"You from around here?"

"Yeah."

"I'm from California."

This didn't impress her. Grady tried to think of something more to say but his mind was like a computer that had lost access to its files. He crumpled his trash and deposited it in the garbage on the way out. He wandered through the crowd for another hour but, despite his feelings of brotherhood, did not make meaningful contact with even a single person. Somehow, there had to be a way to redeem the evening. Nightclubs were expensive and he wouldn't be able to hear over the music, anyway. Something more should have happened, love, friendship, or at least some excitement. Unwilling to give up on the opportunity to make at least one human connection, Grady stayed with the crowd until he realized it was no use. Feeling like he'd missed the president's phone call while buying a Slurpee, Grady made his way back to the apartment on the K Road.

On New Year's Day the cafés on Queen Street were open to service the tourists. Grady and Earl found one that looked acceptable. The waitress sat them at a table next to the bathroom and took their orders.

"Man, I drank too much last night." Earl spilled salt on the table and tried to stand the dispenser on edge. "How about you? What time did you get in?"

"Must have been around two."

"Have a good time?"

"It was all right."

"You hook up with any girls?"

"I did all right."

"That's my boy!"

The waitress brought two café lattes with fern designs in the foam.

"I've been thinking." Earl knocked the saltshaker over and tried again. "If you stayed at home and attended community college, you could work part time at our office. Teach you the ins and outs of defense contracting."

"I don't know."

"Well, think about it. You don't have to decide, today."

The waitress brought their orders. Earl took a bite.

"Miss!" Earl tossed the fork onto his plate. "These eggs are cold!"

"Sorry, sir." The waitress retrieved Earl's plate and passed it through the gap in the wall that opened into the kitchen. "That guy's eggs are cold," she told the cook.

"Excuse me!" Earl said. "I'm not a guy. I'm a customer and I expect to be treated like one!"

Who knows what the cook did with Earl's breakfast? Scrub the toilet? Clean the mold from under the refrigerator? Eventually the eggs returned hot. Earl cut a mouthful with his knife and set it down leaving the tip pointed at his son. It had been a few months since cutlery had bothered Grady but now it made him uneasy. He shifted in his chair so the tip would not point at his heart.

After eating they took the ferry to Waiheke Island. Grady chose seats on the top deck where the wind and diesel noise made conversation impossible. The crossing took less than an hour. After disembarking at the ferry terminal, Grady spotted colorful motor scooters in front of a shed marked, rental.

"This way." Earl pointed to the passengers waiting by a bus.

They rode into town where Grady left his father at a burger stand and went to the beach. Instead of changing into a swimming suit, he merely took off his shoes and let the cold waves lap at his toes. A hundred yards ahead a cluster of black rock formations rose like icebergs from the sand. Grady spent hours wandering among these and exploring tide pools and sea caves before rendezvousing with his father. They returned to Auckland by ferry and got back around 6:00 PM.

Grady got bored with New Zealand's largest city so while Earl was out the next day, he poured through the guidebook and wrote down places he wanted to see: Cape Reinga, the Bay of Islands, Wellington, Rotorua, and the South Island. The big car rental chains had heard of their misadventure in Australia so he called smaller firms. After forty-five minutes on the phone he found one willing to rent Earl a car. Grady made a reservation, scribbled down the details, and waited for his father to return.

Two hours later Earl was still gone and Grady was getting hungry. The refrigerator contained only beer, kiwi fruit, stale bread, and some Vegemite left by a former tenant. Grady walked to an Indian market and bought samosas. Not long after he returned, the phone rang.

"Is this Grady Evans?" a woman asked.

"Yes."

"Can you come to the Auckland Central Police Station? We're holding your father for violation of the Misuse of Drugs Act."

"What? What's this about?"

"It'd be better if we talked at the station. We're at the intersection of Cook and Vincent."

Grady left the takeout bag on the table, ran down the stairs, and dashed onto the sidewalk. As he stepped into the crosswalk, a white Toyota skidded to a stop. Its driver laid on the horn. Grady glared. How satisfying it would be to reach through the window, drag the man who'd thrown up his arms in a gesture of exasperation into the street, and beat him senseless!

"Asshole," Grady muttered through a fake smile, stepped back onto the sidewalk, and let the car pass.

The bus never came. After waiting twenty minutes, Grady wrestled with the map to figure out the route, then gave up and caught a cab instead. The Korean driver made small talk with an accent that sounded as if he had Popsicles in his mouth. When they arrived, Grady paid and walked up the concrete steps.

"I'm Grady Evans. You arrested my father."

"Have a seat," the desk sergeant said. "The constable will be with you shortly."

Grady took a chair next to a Maori man and tried to hide his fascination with the blue lines tattooed on his face. His father's arrest had to be some kind of mistake.

"Sucks. Doesn't it?" Grady's neighbor said.

"Yeah."

A female constable, all blue shirt and efficiency, entered the room.

"Mr. Evans. I'm Constable Galloway. Would you come this way, please?" She led Grady to a windowless room and took a seat across the table from him.

"Has your father been keeping company with any new friends lately?"

"No."

"How about money? Any unexplained sources of income or change in spending habits?"

"Well, he won six hundred dollars gambling in Macau." Grady looked at the constable for approval but she was silent except for the scratch of her pen on paper.

"Have you noticed any personality changes?"

"You mean since my mother died? Yeah, I've noticed a few. Look, what's this all about?"

"Your father tried to fill an Oxycontin prescription for his wife at the Ponsonby Chemists. They called us when a routine check found that Rowan Walker-Evans is in fact dead."

"What happens now?" Grady touched his mother's necklace through the fabric of his shirt. That's why he didn't find her meds when they emptied her suitcase. The old man had them.

"There'll be a bail hearing in District Court after the holiday."

"Bail? You mean you're not going to let him go?"

"We take our drug laws very seriously."

"But…"

Constable Galloway's expression remained as impassive as the Franz Josef Glacier. Grady's entreaties found no purchase.

"Can I see him?" he asked.

"Your father doesn't want visitors right now."

To avoid her eyes Grady studied the insignia and dark epaulettes on her pale blue shirt. Serve and protect! What bullshit! His hair was on fire and that bitch wouldn't even offer him a glass of water. Grady pushed back from the table, raking the linoleum with his chair's legs.

"Anything else?" He stood.

"That will be all for now."

Some kind of pleasantry might have made things smoother but Grady didn't feel like playing the toady. He walked out without another word.

Back at the apartment he rifled the phonebook for lawyers' names. Due to the holiday he reached only answering machines. The legal aid office was open but Grady slammed down the phone after twenty minutes on hold. The pills! What if the police came and found Rowan's pills?

Grady rushed to the bedroom and emptied Earl's suitcase onto the tan carpet. He dug through the pile of golf shirts, Dockers pants, and sweaty white briefs without any luck. Grady searched the side pockets and looked into vitamin bottles. Finally he found Rowan's Oxycontin in Earl's toiletry bag and flushed the pills down the toilet. Did the water swirl the other way north of the equator? He didn't remember.

He tossed the container in the trash, stuffed his father's things back in the suitcase, and heaved it into the bedroom closet. Grady sighed, sat on the easy chair in the living room, and turned on the TV. President Bush was complaining that Saddam wouldn't let weapons inspectors interview scientists without a minder in the room. With his scowl and scared look in his eyes, the president reminded Grady of Dale Van Pelt, a tiny boy in the eighth grade who'd made up for his small size with tough conservative talk. Grady couldn't deal with another international crisis at the moment. The one with his father was enough. He changed to a movie channel.

Gene Hackman was crawling through some jungle, probably in Vietnam. As Hackman crept up on a house built on stilts, a new worry flashed in Grady's brain. What if the police got traces of Oxy from the bottle and used the crime lab report against his father in court?

Grady sprang from the chair and went back to the bathroom. He reached into the plastic trashcan; felt round the used tissues, dental floss, and toilet paper rolls; and retrieved the pill bottle. He rinsed it in the sink. Then with a thumbnail, he peeled the label in curlicues from the plastic. Some paper clung to the bottle's surface but he was confident he'd gotten the part with the printing. He burned the pieces of paper in the kitchen sink, turned on the faucet, and watched the water take the ashes down the drain. Done!

Grady returned to the living room and sat down. He still had five hundred dollars of the cash he'd stolen from his father's money belt. If worse came to worse he could pawn his mother's necklace. Back on the TV, Gene Hackman was wrestling with some villager for control of a machete. Grady thought of the pills again. Fuck it! He took the prescription bottle outside and tossed it in the dumpster. He was too agitated to go back inside so he walked along the K Road, pausing to look in CD shops and used-clothing stores. He had no particular destination but somehow ended up at the aikido dojo he'd trained at on New Year's Eve. The door was open and the teacher now wearing shorts and a T-shirt was using a putty knife to pack spackling compound into a hole in the wall. Grady entered.

"Hi."

"Oh, hey." The teacher pointed to the corner. "Could you get me that sandpaper over there?"

Grady took off his shoes, crossed the mat, and brought a couple sheets to the teacher.

"Thanks. It's the only time I get to patch things up around here." He began to sand the dried spackling, specks of which drifted to the mat. "I love teaching weapons but somebody always puts a *bokken* tip through the wall."

"You need any help?"

"Naw, I got it in hand. So what brings you all the way to N Zed?"

"My dad and I are traveling around the world." Grady pondered how much more to say.

"Lucky bastard! Been to Japan yet?"

"It's the next stop." If his father didn't go to prison, that is.

"Going to train over there?"

"I hope to."

"If you do, say hi to my mate, Doug Turner. Been over at the Hombu Dojo for three or four years."

"And you are?"

"Ben. Ben Dickerson." He extended a hand flecked with dried spackling. "You're Grady, right?"

Grady nodded.

"Be open for class, tomorrow. You're welcome to stop by if you like. Now get out of here. It's too nice a day to spend inside."

The next morning Grady got through to a lawyer and set up an appointment for 2:00 in the afternoon. He'd overreacted the previous day but now everything would be okay. After a leisurely breakfast of muffins, fruit salad, and Earl Grey tea, he bought a Pakeha Pride T-shirt and spent rest of the morning listening to CDs. He arrived at the law office ten minutes early and spent a half hour reading an old issue of Auckland Magazine before the secretary ushered him into the lawyer's office.

R. Timothy Powell was a heavyset man in a gray suit the color of his neatly combed hair. After shaking Grady's hand he sat behind his mahogany desk and asked, "What can I do for you?

"My father's been arrested for trying to buy Oxycontin with my mother's prescription."

"Could he have been buying if for her?" Powell made notes on a yellow legal pad.

"She died last month."

"I'm sorry." Powell set down his gold pen. "Have you talked to him?"

"No."

"Well, it's hard to come up with a defense without talking to your father but we could argue diminished capacity due to your mother's death. I'd better go see him. Where are they holding him?"

"Central Police Station."

"Right." Powell placed his hands together. "Now, there's the small matter of my retainer. I bill a hundred dollars an hour and would need at least ten hour's fee before we can continue."

"My father has all our money." Grady fingered his money belt.

Even with the exchange rate the five hundred dollars inside wouldn't cover the fee, and then how would Grady eat? "Couldn't you just go see him?"

"Have you tried legal aid?" Powell stood from behind the desk and walked Grady to the door. "Gail can give you their number."

"Asshole!" Grady emerged from the elevator on the ground floor and exited the office building. With nothing better to do, he returned to the apartment and called legal aid. Busy! He tried a few other lawyers but they were gone for the extended holiday.

Grady reheated some of the previous night's dinner, got his gi, and headed to the dojo. With all the stress, he hoped the workout wouldn't be too challenging. After Sensei Ben warmed the class up and demonstrated the first technique, Grady turned toward the woman in the black *hakama*. Someone tapped his knee.

"*Onegeishi masu*," It was the guy with the sideburns.

They found an empty spot where Grady countered Sideburns's punches with wobbly *kote gaeshi*. When it was Grady's turn to attack, Sideburns merely stood in place judging Grady was pulling his punches. As he'd suspected Grady's punch was off target.

"Really come for me." Sideburns pointed toward his chest.

Grady had nothing left to lose. He stepped in and thrust his fist forward with all he had. The room spun – wall, ceiling lights, wall, and a slap on the mat. Grady wasn't hurt. He looked down. His body was in perfect position. He'd done it! He had done a break fall! He was a finally real aikidoist! He got up and did it again.

Earl showed up the next day.

"Dad, are you okay?" Grady set his bowl of ramen on the oilcloth covering the kitchen table. "What happened?"

"It's bullshit, Grady!" Earl rushed to the bedroom. "Fuck!" He returned to the kitchen moments later. "I've got to go see my lawyer. Take this in case I don't get back in time for dinner." Earl threw Grady some money. "Hang tight. We'll get through this." Earl clasped Grady behind the neck and brought their foreheads together. Then he left.

Grady poured through Terry Dobson's *Aikido in Everyday Life* in search of a strategy of triangles, circles, and squares that would help with the legal nightmare. He wracked his brain searching for a way to blend with the situation and turn it to his advantage but all he came up with was the square of inaction and triangle of retreat.

Earl spent most days away from the apartment. When he returned at night, he was too stoned, jittery, or sick to eat. Once he even showed up with a cut under his eye. Grady kept away from him by spending as much time as possible at the dojo. Sensei Ben seemed to understand and never asked him to pay.

The following week at his father's request, Grady accompanied him to his lawyer's office. It was located in a modest, three-story office building on Parnell Road. After a fifteen-minute wait, the receptionist showed them in.

"You must be Grady. Your father's told me a lot about you." Mere Whatarau smiled, stood, and shook Grady's hand. She was a heavyset woman with the brown skin and dark hair of her Mauri ancestors. "I think it would be best if Grady and I spoke privately."

"See you back at the apartment." Earl stepped out.

"Please sit." Mere motioned to a chair and examined some papers on her desk. "Would you care for coffee?"

Grady shook his head.

"You may be called to testify at your father's trial. We need to talk so I'll know what you're going to say. Please be honest. Any surprises could damage your father's defense. Do you have any questions?"

Grady shook his head.

"Right. Let's begin. Were you aware of your father's drug use before his arrest?"

"No."

"Are you aware of any evidence that could be used against him?"

Grady stared at her. Should he mention the pills he flushed down the toilet? No, it was best to forget it ever happened. He shook his head.

"Good." Mere folded her hands and leaned forward. "The facts of the case aren't in dispute. I'm going to argue that your father is a decent man who turned to drugs because he was overcome with grief. Judges have been known to be lenient in similar cases. I want you to paint me a picture of what your father was like before your mother died."

"Well, he didn't beat me or anything." Grady thought about the Dutch prostitute, the arguments, and how Earl had manipulated him into postponing college. "He was a good provider, I guess."

"Grady, I'm counting on you to convince the judge your father's a good man. Surely, you must have some happy memories to share."

The room was silent except for the faint tick of a clock. Grady stared at the desk. What could he say in defense of the grumpy guy he'd shared a house with for eighteen years? Grady wasn't even sure he liked the man but he had to say something.

"Going to work every day to feed your family is not a trivial thing!" Grady raised his voice to convey a passion he did not feel. "My dad busted his ass to provide a good life for me."

"Of course. Let's move on. Shall we? If you think of anything more, please let me know."

They talked for another half hour about how Earl fell apart after Rowan's death. At the end of the interview, Mere thanked Grady and promised to be in touch. He took the bus home.

Grady never had to testify. In exchange for a guilty plea, the Crown fined Earl five thousand dollars and expelled him from the country. This was cheaper than incarceration and freed the government from paying for Earl's rehab.

On a Thursday morning, Grady found himself sitting beside his father in the international terminal of Auckland's airport. Two beefy New Zealand policemen in caps with checkered bands sat with arms crossed on either side of them. Not only did these humorless men refuse to laugh at Earl's jokes but they also denied him the chance to shop for souvenirs. After the other passengers took their seats, Grady and Earl boarded the plane bound for Tokyo. Their escorts remained at the gate until the flight attendants sealed the doors.

"Fuck it!" Earl buckled his seatbelt. "If you don't get thrown out of at least one country, you're just not trying."

Grady paged through the in-flight magazine during the emergency exit/oxygen mask drill. After taxiing to the runway, the pilot spooled the engines and released the brakes. The giant hand of inertia pressed Grady into his seat. The plane pitched nose up, and the ground fell away beneath them. Grady looked through the window for a last glimpse of the city of sails. They would fly over thousands of miles of ocean before crossing land.

CHAPTER 15

While he and his father stood in an immigration line that snaked between portable barriers at Tokyo's Narita Airport, Grady placed his arrival card in the picture page of his passport.

"I've been thinking." Earl fumbled in his pocket for his documents. "With the situation in New Zealand and all, we're ahead of schedule. Suppose we caught a flight to Bangkok? It's cheap there. We could kick around Southeast Asia for a few months, fly to Seoul, and catch a boat back to Japan when it's warmer. Hell, we could even go to Vietnam."

"What will we do there?"

"What will we do?" Earl chuckled. "We'll live like kings! That's what we'll do!"

"We could catch a plane home." Grady lowered his voice. "And get you into a drug treatment program."

"Quiet." Earl's voice changed to a whisper as he cast a nervous look at the immigration officers. "We'll talk about this later."

An officer motioned to the huge Polynesian woman in front of them. They were next up. Like so many times before Grady stood behind a yellow line on the floor and waited to be called. He'd crossed a lot of boundaries on his journey – borders between nations, the line separating childhood from the disappointing world of adults, and the boundary to the land of grief. He'd even escorted his mother to the edge of death, a country that would remain unexplored by him for years to come. Previously he would have been tempted to inch his toe across the line on the floor but that was before he'd learned to recognize the value of boundaries. Sometimes you weren't meant to cross. All those other passengers had waited behind the lines not out of fear but out of courtesy. Or maybe like him, they were just tired.

The immigration officer motioned them forward, stamped their passports, and sent them on their way. Grady and his father rolled their bags past customs and through the sliding glass doors that opened into the terminal. A dozen Japanese greeters in winter coats held up cardboard signs for arriving passengers: Mr. Harry Paulson, Dr. Margaret Smith, etc. Grady and Earl passed them and then stopped. The other passengers flowed around them like a stream around boulders.

"I'm going to check on flights to Thailand. Wait here." Earl rolled his bag a few steps and turned. "It's going to be wild, Grady. Just wait and see."

Grady watched his father walk under a hanging, black display that listed departing flights in glowing red lettering and then board the escalator.

Four hours later Grady got off the subway at Shinjuku Station and stood trying to decide which exit to take in the seething mass of commuters. He chose at random, left through the ticket booth, and followed the crowd outside. There, he stood shivering while looking at the map. The hoody and hemp jacket he wore were not thick enough to shield him from the January cold. Uniformed school children and salarymen in overcoats rushed in all directions like ants whose nest had been kicked. A woman's face took up a billboard across the street. A huge screen showed video footage of antiwar protestors carrying signs saying, "No blood for oil," "Do not attack Iraq," and "Not in my name." There appeared to be thousands.

Grady placed a finger on the map and looked at street signs to see which exit he'd taken. Had he done the right thing? After his father had walked away, Grady had hopped a JR train from the airport to Tokyo Station and booked one of those coffin-sized rooms in a capsule hotel. If he watched his spending, his money might hold out for ten days. That Doug guy had better be at the dojo.

"May I help you?" asked a middle-aged Japanese man whose British-accented English sounded out of place to Grady. He was short and wore a camel-colored overcoat.

"I'm trying to get to the Aikido Hombu Dojo." Grady handed him a pamphlet with the address.

"Hombu Dojo. Hombu Dojo." The man stroked his chin. "Wakamatsu cho! Eh? Okay, if you pay my bus fare, I'll take you."

They boarded a bus and Grady handed a five-hundred-yen note to the white-gloved driver. The middle-aged man led Grady to a pair of empty seats behind two high school girls who wore identical, dark coats and giggled at the pictures in their books. Periodically someone would pull the cord that sounded a bell and lit a sign with characters that Grady couldn't read. Conversation with the middle-aged man was awkward so Grady looked out the window at the ubiquitous pachinko parlors with their garish decorations. Nothing natural was visible, only a limitless expanse of concrete and high rises with signs in *kanji* hanging from various floors. He sure hoped the stranger didn't rob him.

"Okay, this is our stop." The man hustled out the door. Grady followed.

"*Sumimasen.*" The man approached an old lady with a cloth mask over her nose and mouth. He fired off a stream of Japanese punctuated with the words Aikido Hombu Dojo. The woman replied while pointing down the street.

"*Hai. Hai. Hai,*" the man said.

She said some more and pointed left.

"*Arigato gozaimasu.*" The man bowed to the woman. "Okay, this way." He led Grady down the sidewalk and turned off the main road onto side streets surrounded by apartment buildings.

Grady's patron questioned a red-faced young man with surprised eyebrows and a teenage girl with spiky pink hair before leading him to an unpretentious, concrete building.

"Aikido Hombu Dojo. Thank you very much." The stranger shook Grady's hand and walked away.

Inside two brawny Caucasians, one dark-haired and the other blonde, ambled down the stairs carrying gym bags. In the corner was an office set off by a Dutch door. The top half was open. Grady approached. A balding man in a white shirt and khaki slacks set his cup of tea down on the desk and handed him a form and a pencil with teeth marks near the eraser. Grady examined the document, written in both Japanese and English. It was an application to become a student. He touched the pencil to paper and began with the easy part, his name. He was Grady Walker-Evans.

ABOUT THE AUTHOR

Host of the Gelato Poetry Series and an editor of the *San Diego Poetry Annual*, Jon Wesick has published hundreds of poems and stories in small press journals. He is the author of the novel *Hunger for Annihilation* and the poetry collection *Words of Power, Dances of Freedom*.

Made in the USA
Charleston, SC
24 October 2015